# Cottonwood Dreams

Book Three of the Prairie Pastor Series

Gayle Larson Schuck

***Cottonwood Dreams***
Copyright © 2021 Gayle Larson Schuck



All scripture references are from the New International Version Bible unless otherwise noted.

Cover photo by Paulette Bullinger
Cover design by Carrie Peters: https://cheekycovers.com


**Also by Gayle Larson Schuck:**
*By the Banks of Cottonwood Creek,* the first book in the Prairie Pastor Series
*Amber's Choice,* the second book in the Prairie Pastor Series
*Secrets of the Dark Closet,* a historical novel

*Many thanks to the following people:*

The Wordsmiths writers group. Your weekly encouragement, get-real feedback, and friendship keep me going.

Patricia Olson, Linda Lewis, Korrine Lang and Cinnamon Schuck for editing and proofreading the manuscript. Your time, talent, skill and support mean so much.

John Maddock, who wrote "Cottonwoods." John, who I've known most of my adult life, invited me to join a local writers group. Now 90 years young, he continues to be a role model.

Miranda Stanley for the photo shoot.

Nancy Rumney for the description of Brianna's wedding dress.

Fellow travelers on the Farmer's Union trip to Texas in January 2019. Your stories about small-town life and farming provided authentic details for this story.

To my husband, Larry, for believing in me.

This book was completed on the wings of prayer. Thank you to friends and family who often sent up prayers, and "happened" to encourage me at just the right time.

And to my savior and friend, Jesus Christ. Your Word is indeed a lamp to my feet and a light to my path.

Isaiah 61:1-3

The Spirit of the Sovereign Lord is on me,
because the Lord has anointed me
to proclaim good news to the poor.
He has sent me to bind up the brokenhearted,
to proclaim freedom for the captives
and release from darkness for the prisoners,
to proclaim the year of the Lord's favor
and the day of vengeance of our God,
to comfort all who mourn,
and provide for those who grieve in Zion—
to bestow on them a crown of beauty
instead of ashes,
the oil of joy
instead of mourning,
and a garment of praise
instead of a spirit of despair.
They will be called oaks of righteousness,
a planting of the Lord
for the display of his splendor.

*"Keep your face to the sunshine and you cannot see the shadows. It's what sunflowers do."* -- Helen Keller

**What readers say about the Prairie Pastor Series:**

*"I read all of your books. I loved all of them and wondered if you have more. Do you? I'm impatiently waiting."*
– Rita, North Dakota

*"A captivating read from beginning to end."*
– Linda, Michigan

*"I read it in one sitting. Should be a warning label on it that once u start reading u WILL NOT lay aside till finished."*
– Isabelle, North Dakota

*"We read it slowly to savor it longer. What a great read!"*
– Paul, Colorado

*"A love story on many levels."*
– Sandi, Minnesota

*"A heart-warming story of friendship, love & faith."*
– Barbara, Illinois

*"Lots of good food for thought for young people reading this romance. Also the career/family issue speaks to many."*
– Jordis, North Dakota

Chapter 1

# A Place to Belong

Brianna Davis gripped her suitcase in one hand and her sewing machine in the other as she looked up at the tall stately house that would be her new home. It resembled the Painted Lady mansions she'd left behind in San Francisco. However, when she looked beyond the house instead of a view of the Bay, she saw a wide lawn with gardens and beyond that a cornfield.

The sign on the way into town read, "Welcome to Schulteville. We're Glad You Are Here." Brianna planned to embrace that greeting. Setting down her things, she stretched her muscles. Her Miata was fine for short trips, but thousands of miles of Interstate put her long legs to sleep.

Brianna wanted to be known for her work in design, even as she risked working remotely from halfway across the country. *There's more to me than meets the eye*, her oft-quoted motto went through her mind. Her tall, slender figure, olive complexion and flowing dark hair had caused her plenty of trouble. She hoped by moving here that her looks would no longer define her.

Sighing, she focused on the maize color and the architecture of the Queen Anne house. The house begged to be made into a bed and breakfast, and that's what Brianna planned to do. When the owner, Kate Schulte, proposed the idea, it had immediately seized Brianna's imagination. Now the elderly Kate and youthful Brianna planned to be the proprietors of Kate's Bed & Breakfast.

Of course, it needed a fair amount of redecorating and some remodeling first. Still, the house was the most outstanding building in town. Brianna planned to make it a destination. *Lady, you are going to be so happy when I give you a makeover.*

When her phone buzzed in her hip pocket, Brianna fished it out.

"Hey, hey, when you gonna come inside?"

"Tiny? What are you doing here?" Brianna asked as she spied him through the front window. Tiny Winger, the other reason she'd moved across the country. Her heart warmed to think he had driven over from Cottonwood City to welcome her.

Then the screen door flew open, and all of her favorite North Dakota people spilled out, like a cast of characters coming on stage. First, Amber Jorgenson skipped down the steps, arms open wide for a hug. Kelly leaned on the railing of the wraparound porch, wearing a big smile. Kate Schulte clomped out with her cane. Marge and Wayne Selby, who lived with Kate and helped care for her, brought up the rear.

Everyone began talking at once. How was her trip? Had she eaten lunch? Could they help unload her car? Then, the chatter dropped off as Tiny approached.

At five-foot-ten, she was several inches shorter than he, but tall enough to look into his velvety blue eyes. After they met a few months ago at Kelly and Amber's wedding, her life began changing radically.

*Like Alice in Wonderland,* Brianna thought, *I slipped into a hole and found another world.* Of course, she had stepped into a gopher hole that day rather than a rabbit hole. Still, the life she discovered here was no less surprising and enchanting than if she'd found herself in Wonderland.

"You're here!" Tiny said, his arms frozen to his sides.

"I am," Brianna agreed. They continued to grin at each other like two Cheshire cats.

Kate coughed and called out, "Can't you cut to the chase and kiss her?"

When the others chuckled, Tiny's ears turned a charming pink. An uncomfortable silence followed, as the couple continued to stare at one another.

Kelly finally broke the tension. "My turn, Buddy," he said as he clapped Tiny on the shoulder and pushed him out of the way. Then he embraced Brianna in a bear hug.

"Welcome to your new home, old friend. I hope you find happiness here as I have."

Over Kelly's shoulder, Brianna winked at Tiny. The big Scandinavian's shyness would never allow him to kiss her in front of others. Heck, he'd never kissed her when they were alone.

Brianna's heart warmed even more. After a lifetime of refined, smooth-talking men, Tiny's unvarnished awkwardness and sincerity drew her to him. The rest of the world might overlook his charms, but she found them most appealing.

Aunt Kate clapped her hands. "Marge has refreshments for us. Let's move inside," she said in her best school superintendent voice. The others filed past her as if a class bell had rung.

"How are you, Bri?" Tiny asked as they stood alone, face to face.

"I might dream about bugs on the windshield tonight." She mimicked steering her car.

"You drove across the mountains by yourself. I haven't done nothing like that."

Brianna smoothed out her tunic, feeling a little rumpled. "You look great. Thank you for being here to greet me."

"Aw, it's nothing." He fidgeted, moving from one foot to another. "Would, would you like to go out with me tomorrow night? I think we should have some fun and celebrate."

"Yes!" Brianna pictured an Italian restaurant she'd seen in Bismarck and thought that would be the perfect place to celebrate a new life.

Memories of another invitation captured her thoughts for a moment. She'd been the arm candy of an executive for a holiday dinner aboard a yacht. She wore a little red satin dress and a diamond necklace. She'd hoped to make some business contacts, but that hadn't happened. What she remembered was the sloshing cocktails, designer drugs, and dining after midnight. Oh, yes, and the forced laughter.

The party had depressed her. Then, the next week her business partner, Jontel, had temporarily moved to Sweden. She'd spent Christmas alone. Truly alone. Desperate, she had reached out to her old friend Kelly, and he helped her find hope.

Tiny looked into her eyes and her heart speeded up. "Would you like to go bowling?" he asked, uncertainly. "It's a really nice bowling alley."

Brianna swallowed. "Bowling? You mean where you roll a ball toward some pins?" Brianna looked at her long nails, done in the latest shimmering coral. *Bowling balls break nails.*

Tiny's grin lit up his whole face. She'd forgotten how his blonde hair curled at the base of his neck. "I'll teach you how to bowl. And, hey, they have the best corndogs in the state."

She looked at his sweet, handsome face. How could she refuse? *Goodbye Italian restaurant, hello bowling alley.*

"Okay. Learning to bowl sounds like fun. But, Tiny, I will never, ever eat a corndog."

"Don't like 'em?"

"Not the name. Not the taste. Not whatever they put in them."

Tiny's face fell. "Have you ever tried one?"

"No and I won't. Can we find a quiet restaurant where we can talk, instead?"

Tiny shrugged. "Sure. It's a deal."

When he took her hand, she remembered the executive who had held her hand and suggestively kissed her wrist. *What will Tiny do?* She wondered. Instead of kissing her hand, he shook it.

Brianna flung her arms around him and squeezed him tightly. Now his whole face turned pink as he squeezed back.

"Tiny, I'm so happy to be here." She'd wear jeans to go bowling, but some night, some special night, she was going to show up on a date in the little red satin dress and watch Tiny's ears smoke.

He disengaged himself and then, looking toward her car he snorted. "How did you drive that jellybean across the United States?" He set down her things and went to examine her tiny red convertible. "It only has two seats! Not much of a trunk."

Brianna laughed. "Now don't scoff at my Miata. It's very reliable."

"Better trade it in on something practical before winter," he advised. "You won't get through the snow and ice with a rear-wheel drive."

He hoisted her suitcase and sewing machine for the trip into the house. "What's this contraption?" he asked.

"My sewing machine. I'll need it before the moving van brings the rest of my things. I brought some fabric, too. I'm going to make new window treatments for the bed and breakfast."

"You sew things? No way. Mom likes to sew, too."

"Tiny, I've been sewing since I was ten years old." *There's so much we don't know about each other.*

She sighed. For a moment she wondered if coming here was the right thing to do. Many people thought she was leaving an enviable life.

Still, she couldn't stand her soulless existence anymore. Her life had been as cold and hard as the industrial design concepts that were so popular. Concrete counters. Steel walls. White floors. They called it a clean look, but she thought it was barren of personality. After coming to North Dakota a year ago, she had incorporated sunflowers into her designs in rebellion against the starkness.

She gazed up at the Queen Anne house. It had soul! She wouldn't put one piece of cold hard metal in that house. Going into business with Kate Schulte was an edgy thing to do. Turning this old house into a bed and breakfast was the boldest step she'd ever taken.

The decision beat in her heart like the wings of a bird about to take off. *Wings of hope* she thought. *I have wings of hope.*

"This is a place to call home," she whispered. She would adapt to bowling balls, chilly falls, and snowballs.

Tiny had delivered her baggage and now turned to hold out his hand. She took it as Kate opened the door wide in welcome.

Chapter 2

# Brianna's Nightmare

*Brianna flicked off the hall light as she slipped into the blackness of the bedroom. There wasn't even a shaft of light to guide her. She felt for the cool smooth surface of the dresser and found it. Her hand trailed along the edge as she moved toward the bed. When the scent of musky shaving lotion wafted through the air, she froze in fear. Someone was in the room with her.*

She startled into wakefulness, her heart beating hard. Then, she realized she was safely tucked between the soft old sheets in her new room in the turret of Kate Schulte's home. The grandfather clock ticked comfortingly from the floor below. *It's only the nightmare,* she told herself.

Her fear seemed to leave through the wall like a departing aberration. Still, the irony of the nightmare brought tears to her eyes. She was ready for a new beginning, surrounded by friends, far away from the city and her former life. Why did the nightmare have to follow her?

She was barely in her teens when boys and men started paying special attention to her. She was sometimes mistaken for a famous Hollywood starlet because of her olive skin and dark eyes. Most recently, a well-dressed, but creepy, man in San Francisco started appearing at the stand where she bought her morning coffee. The way he brushed against her had made her want to whap him with her handbag. Even now, her resentment flared.

Did he wear musk-scented shaving lotion? No, he hadn't. She began having the nightmare before he was around. There was enough in her past to cause nightmares. The memory of Kyle dying in her arms. Before that, a childhood filled with anxiety from often changing schools. All those cocktail parties her parents hosted. Oh yeah, and those impossible standards her mother had set.

The waning moon cast soft light on a wall hanging. From beneath a downy quilt, she could make out just a few words: "a garment of praise for a spirit of heaviness." The rest of the saying was lost in the shadows, but she was familiar with the scripture.

Someone had said faith was like a muscle. The more you use it, the stronger it grows. At times like these she wished her courage and faith had more muscle.

Her eyes stayed on the wall hanging. The saying was based on Isaiah 61. God promised to replace her grief and despair with joy. To give her a garment of praise for the spirit of heaviness. However, there was more to it. She needed to wrap herself in a garment of praise.

In the stillness of the coming dawn, her voice sounded as weak as a small child's in an empty room. However, the tension of the nightmare began to fade as she hummed a praise song and peace enveloped her.

Grateful, she wiped her eyes with the edge of her silk pajamas. Then she began thanking God for her friends, Kelly and Amber Jorgenson. For Wayne and Marge, who would surely help strengthen her faith through their love and care. For Kate Schulte, who had taken her in as a friend and business partner. And for Tiny. Especially for Tiny. Kelly called him a diamond in the rough, and she had to agree with his assessment.

Her first impression of him was not good. They were both at Kelly and Amber's wedding. She evaluated his brown suit, high water pants and flip-flops, and categorized him as an overweight country hick.

Her second impression happened when she broke her ankle right after the wedding. He'd been roped into taking her to the emergency room in Bismarck. That day he'd been grudgingly gracious and more than able to help her. That tweaked her view a bit. Still, he was obsessed with food and socially clumsy.

Brianna knew, as women always do, that he had a crush on her. That was nothing new. What was different was that he didn't try to hit on her. He remained calm and polite during all the hours they were together, despite her admittedly crabby mood.

Unable to fly back to California, she had spent a couple weeks at Kate Schulte's until she had medical clearance to fly again. During that time, Tiny had stayed away, and Brianna's conscience nagged her.

Months later, Amber had a serious car accident and Brianna had returned to help during the critical days that followed. Her perfectly glossed mouth had dropped open when Tiny appeared at the airport to pick her up when she returned to North Dakota. He was taller than she remembered. Leaner. More confident.

Their friendship began that day, with a heartfelt apology from Brianna.

Enough thinking, Brianna decided. It was the first full day of her new life in Schulteville, and she planned to enjoy it. She rose and donned her running clothes for an early morning jog. In minutes, she was beyond the Schulteville city limits and immersed in nature.

Flocks of geese were noisily rising in the dawn to fly south for the winter. From a distance, they seemed so graceful. Then several geese suddenly flapped unceremoniously from the ditch to her right. They were so close that she let out a shriek, while they honked their annoyance with her. *This must be a country-style traffic jam*, she thought.

Then, a seam of gold creased the eastern horizon, the crimson curtain went up, and the sun rose in an alleluia chorus of color.

The fields of sunflowers glowed in the early morning light. Their round flower faces were speckled with black seeds, their yellow bonnets faded. They faced east like a vast auditorium of sunflower people waiting for the miracle of a new day.

Brianna stopped to catch her breath and drink in the scene. It was now utterly quiet except for the honking of birds whimsically moving across the sky. Sunflowers had inspired her design work since she first visited North Dakota. Now, this place became her broader inspiration with its peace, muted autumn colors, and the minute details of each flower and spear of grass.

Finally, regretfully, she turned back toward town, pledging to make this run every morning until the winter prevailed.

It was Sunday and an unusually warm day for October. At breakfast, Kate asked Brianna to take her to church in the Miata that morning. With the top down. Brianna liked the idea. Since she was already attracting a lot of attention, she might as well take advantage of it. Perhaps, their arrival together would help remind people that they were opening a bed and breakfast. They could use some free advertising.

She had caused a stir when she visited the church a year ago. Everyone thought she was Pastor Kelly's girlfriend. She remembered the pain on Kelly's face when he had to explain that Brianna had dated his twin brother who had been killed.

Now, Brianna enjoyed the freedom of stepping on the gas and breezing across the open prairie. Kate and Brianna did draw plenty of attention when they drove up. At eighty-eight, Kate needed help dislodging herself from the tiny car. Brianna retrieved her cane, and arm in arm, hair askew from the ride, they made their way up the church steps and into the sanctuary.

Kate's seat in the front row was guaranteed. It was general knowledge that Kate was cantankerous enough to rap people on the ankle with her cane if they took her seat.

All eyes followed them as they made their way up the aisle. Kate was wearing an outdated, but perfectly good, yellow suit. Brianna looked like a fashion model in her sleek black and white suit. Amber smiled at them from the pew where the choir sat.

Kelly was at the podium going through his notes as the piano wrapped up a song. Brianna noted that a look of surprise and mirth crossed Kelly's face when he glanced up and saw them. He quickly looked down again.

*He's trying to compose himself*, Brianna thought. Did they look that funny? Was there toilet paper sticking to her shoe? An open zipper?

She again glanced at Amber, who smiled reassuringly. It was then that Brianna realized what an odd pair she and Kate made. *Two brassy women headed for the front row.*

The last note of piano music died out and a guitar began strumming. "All rise for the reading from Psalm 92, verses one through four," Kelly explained before he began to read:

*"It is good to praise the LORD and make music to your name, O Most High, proclaiming your love in the morning and your faithfulness at night, to the music of the ten-stringed lyre and the melody of the harp. For you make me glad by your deeds, Lord; I sing for joy at what your hands have done."*

*"Let us praise the Lord together by singing the hymn found on page 368."*

The guitar grew louder as the piano joined in again. Then, as one, the people began to sing together.

Brianna's heart swelled as the music rose. Since she

had made a simple declaration of faith the year before, she'd attended a small Bible study in her neighborhood, but had never found a church home.

Yet, here in Cottonwood Church, they were singing a song she often heard on Christian television programs. Kelly had read a familiar scripture. Looking around, she realized she had as many friends here as she did in California.

Sure, she drew attention in this rural community. She seemed strange to them and their ways seemed strange to her, but the people she knew here were genuine friends.

"My hope is based on nothing less than Jesus' blood and righteousness," the congregation sang boisterously. Brianna remained silent, her thoughts going back to the phenomenal sunrise that morning. *Sun. Son,* she thought.

It seemed that the Son was rising in her life, bringing light and hope. She found her voice as they came to the chorus. "On Christ the solid rock I stand. All other ground is sinking sand, all other ground is sinking sand."

*For the first time ever, I feel like I'm on solid ground,* she thought. *I want to build my life here.*

# Chapter 3

# *First Date*

Brianna and Tiny began their first date with a stop at the Prairie Rose Diner for dinner. Tiny explained that by nine o'clock the bowling alley would be the only place open in town. She recalled that corndogs were their specialty, so the diner sounded like a great option.

Business peaked at the diner earlier in the day. By evening, a relaxed crowd of single men and retired couples took most of the seats. When Tiny and Brianna walked in, conversation stopped. All eyes followed the self-conscious couple as they strolled across the room.

Once they found a booth in a corner, the noise level picked up again. Brianna had dressed casually, but now her only pair of jeans, low riders with a studded belt, seemed upscale. Perhaps she shouldn't have tucked in her white t-shirt or pulled on her cute blue denim boots.

"I think they're looking at me," Brianna murmured.

"That's because you look great," Tiny whispered as he waved to a couple at a nearby table. They wiggled their fingers back and then concentrated on their food.

"They'll get used to seeing you around. Hey, maybe I should introduce you." He started to stand up, but Brianna tugged at his arm.

"No!" she said, shaking her head.

Tiny shrugged her off. "Hey, can I have everyone's attention? This here is Brianna Davis. She just moved here. She and Kate Schulte are turning Kate's house into a bed and breakfast over in Schulteville. I hope you'll make her welcome."

Brianna's eyes were wide with mortification. Several people waved or called out a greeting. Others just chewed their food and stared. She smiled weakly and waved.

"That wasn't really necessary," she muttered into her menu.

The menu was short on vegetables and long on carbs. Special of the Day: Chicken-fried steak and mashed potatoes. It also included the restaurant's deluxe Massive burger, deep-fried fish and a loaded baked potato. The salad choice in the bottom right-hand corner of the menu seemed like an afterthought: Tossed salad, macaroni and cheese salad, and coleslaw.

"I quit ordering Massive burgers when I decided to lose weight," Tiny confided. "Otherwise, I mostly just eat less. No Massive burgers and no extra helpings. I still treat myself, though. Sometimes I order off the breakfast menu."

"Oh, that's a good idea." A memory brought a smile to her lips.

When the waitress came for their order, Tiny ordered hash browns, one egg, toast and a glass of milk. "Switched from soda to milk," he explained to Brianna. "Better for the bones."

After ordering a pancake with bacon strips and a side of applesauce, she said, "When I was growing up, sometimes we'd have breakfast for dinner. Mom would slice up fruit and lecture me about the four food groups, but Daddy mixed up chocolate pancake batter and made pancake bears."

"Sounds like you had a great childhood."

"Yes, I guess I did," Brianna said, but her eyes clouded. Shrugging, she changed the subject. "Why don't you tell me about the finer points of bowling?"

When they arrived at the bowling alley, Brianna caused a stir again. However, overall, the bowling date went well.

On the way home, Tiny told her, "You're a natural with a bowling ball! I've been looking for a partner. Would you like to join a couple's league with me?"

Brianna smiled and frowned at the same time, a habit her mother had tried hard to break. Bowling hadn't been too bad, except for losing a fingernail. Joining a league for couples was another matter. She didn't think of them as a couple, yet, although she suspected the rest of the county would have them engaged by the end of the week.

"I thought you and Kelly bowled together."

"We do, but now that he's married, Amber has him on a leash. Besides, he always has his nose stuck in his books."

*Amber has Kelly on a leash? This guy is a real he-man.* She could give him a speech on respect and women's rights, but somehow she didn't want to. He hadn't said it in a condescending way. It was more likely a way to say Kelly and Amber were a team. "Kelly must be pretty serious about studying."

"Yep. That's why he has great sermons. He's always digging out new truths for us."

They were almost to Schulteville now, and Brianna wondered how the date would end. Too often, she ended up defending herself on dates, but that didn't seem likely with Tiny. *Maybe he'll shake hands again,* she thought. *Disclaimer: I'm not opposed to a goodnight kiss.*

"It's supposed to be a pretty nice day on Sunday. Would you like to go hiking down at Cross Ranch State Park?"

"Would I ever!" *He asked me on another date. That's better than a kiss.*

The pickup rolled to a stop in front of Kate's house. The porch light flicked on. They sat in awkward silence for a moment.

"I like your pickup." Amber had confided that Tiny had cleaned up his rig before the date. Now, she coyly added, "Did you shine it up for me?"

A man without guile, Tiny looked at her and nodded. "I didn't want you to ruin your pretty clothes by sitting on grease rags."

The porch lights blinked off and back on. *I need to remind Kate that I'm an adult.*

"Thank you. That was very sweet. You're a pretty nice guy."

Tiny looked stricken and then took a deep breath. "Well, Kate chewed me out. Said I needed to clean up my pickup before taking you anywhere."

"Oh, Tiny. That was mean of her. You know, I like you just the way you are."

"I don't understand why. But I'm real honored that you do."

Brianna reached over and took Tiny's big hand in hers, feeling the calloused roughness. She longed to build a relationship and talk about things deeper than traveling or bowling. However, before she could let her heart spill out, the porch lights blinked off and on, off and on.

"Guess I better walk you to the door or Kate will be out here with her .22." Tiny reached for his door handle but turned back to Brianna. "We have a date on Sunday?"

"Yes. I can't wait."

Chapter 4

# Cross Roads at Cross Ranch

**B**rianna admired the splendor of the October day as she and Tiny drove south on Highway 83. They planned to spend Sunday afternoon at Cross Ranch State Park.

The autumn landscape was painted a golden hue. Fields of sunflowers and corn, with stalks as high as a man, stretched to the horizon. The sea of land washed against the vast sky, opening the soul to consider the breadth of eternity.

From her previous trips, Brianna remembered the giant power plants that were in sight of the highway. By contrast, nearby trucks and train cars looked like miniature toys. Close by, black cattle stood like polka dots against golden pastures.

Turning off at Washburn, they followed a quiet road to a square brown sign announcing the entrance to Cross Ranch State Park. When they got out of the pickup, Brianna noticed the same hush that had filled the air during her early morning run. She looked up at the lacy gold and orange canopy formed by the giant trees. Layers of dried leaves covered the terrain.

"Outstanding!" she said, turning in a circle. "But where are the people?"

Tiny surveyed the vehicles in the parking lot and shrugged. "People are here, but there are miles of trails. We might not see anybody else."

They wandered over to the river. "The Mighty Missouri," Tiny explained. "Also known as the Muddy Missouri and, when it floods, it becomes the Misery River."

Brianna shook her head and whispered, "It's immense." She couldn't take her eyes off the river as they found a log and sat down. She studied the bottle green water. Looking across the wide expanse, it seemed tranquil, but leaves and small twigs tumbled along near the shore. Watching closely, she could see the swift force of the water.

She noticed an island far from shore that was filled with brush and trees. A movement caught her eye as two deer stepped into a clearing on the island.

"Look," she whispered and pointed at the tawny pair.

Tiny raised his hands as though pointing a gun and pretended to pull the trigger.

"Oh no!" Brianna cried out. "They're so beautiful. You wouldn't shoot them."

She paused. "Would you?"

"You bet. I go deer hunting every year."

"That's just wrong!"

"You won't say that after one of those stupid animals forgets to look both ways and smashes into your car."

Brianna was appalled. *This man is not eco-friendly.*

"Tell you what, I'll make deer sausage for supper some night."

She scooted a few inches away from Tiny. *If he thinks I'd eat deer meat, he doesn't know me at all. But wait, was that an invitation to dinner at his house? Maybe I could meet his mother. I wonder if she's anything like Amber's mom? But, I couldn't go. I'm getting back on my highly nutritional culinary supplements whenever my order arrives.*

Tiny continued a bit defensively, "I have a great sausage recipe."

Brianna decided to change the subject before an argument broke out. Leaning over, she scooped up a handful of the fine sand and let it run through her fingers. "This is like ocean sand."

"Yep. It's a nice beach, but it isn't a good place to swim. Even in the warmest months, the river stays at about fifty-five degrees. It's better to go fishing."

"Kelly said he went fishing with you."

"Yep. Amber likes to fish, too. Maybe we can all go next year. I have a little boat that we take up to Lake Audubon, north of Cottonwood City."

"I'd like that," she said, bravely, thankful that it was too late in the season to go now.

"We can fry up some fish afterward."

Brianna frowned. The word "fried" was not in her culinary vocabulary.

They decided to wander through the mixed prairie grass that made up much of the park. Sometimes the great river was their companion, and sometimes they were lost in the forest.

"This is incredible," she said as she piled through a carpet of golden cottonwood leaves and grabbed a post to steady herself. The uneven trail had thrown her off balance. Her ankle was still healing from the fall she had taken at Amber and Kelly's wedding.

"It looks like it did when Lewis and Clark were here a couple hundred years ago. They say this is the only natural stretch along the whole river. Most of it has been dammed up."

"I'm so glad they left this as it was," Briana declared. "I grew up in suburbs. Manicured lawns. Paved streets. This brings out a love for the wildness that I didn't know I had."

"Maybe under all that polish you're a redneck at heart."

*This prissy city girl? Not a chance.* Still, the thought made her smile.

"Tiny, can we go somewhere and just talk?"

"Sure. Let's drive around." They followed the path for a long way, and finally Tiny took Brianna's elbow and steered her toward the pickup.

"Oh look!" Brianna exclaimed as she climbed in. The setting sun was framed by tall, rough tree trunks, their branches forming an arch over the top of the picture.

"Have you ever seen anything prettier? Can we stay and watch the sun go down?"

As they sat mesmerized by the view, she asked, "Do you come here often?"

"When I can get away for a few hours. Back when I was a kid, a neighbor asked me to go fishing here with their family. He brought a fishing pole for me, baited my hook and helped me untangle my line. Hey, that was a good time."

"One town, one school, always knew your neighbors," Brianna said in wonder. "We moved so many times. I don't even remember any neighbors."

"Where were you born?"

"In Houston. Then we moved to Cincinnati, Chicago, Atlanta, back to Houston. Let's see, we spent a summer in Wilmington, Delaware. Then, when I was a freshman in high school, we settled in Huntington Beach. That was home until my parents moved from there."

"Gee, I don't think I'd like that. Were you an Army brat?"

"No," Brianna sighed. "Daddy is with a large corporation and he likes to move around. Helena—my mother doesn't want to be called 'Mom'—insisted that we stay in one place while I finished high school. Then off they went. They're in England now."

Brianna continued, "I was an only child and always the new kid at school. Helena was a big supporter of the arts. She enrolled me in every possible creative class to keep me busy."

"I was an only child, too, but my mother never enrolled me in anything."

As they sat looking at the sunset, Brianna felt so close to Tiny, as though they had always been friends. Her emotions welled up and she wanted to bare her soul, to tell him all about her life, her hopes, her every thought.

"Tiny, I think you should know that you don't know who I am, because I don't know who I am. I'm a person in transition and I don't know who I'm becoming, but I'm not who I was. I think I'm just beginning to find myself by moving here. Does that make sense?" she asked.

He frowned and squinted. "Nope."

There was a long moment of silence and then Brianna began giggling.

"Are you laughing at me?" he asked.

"No. I'm laughing at us." She laughed harder, snorted, and then covered her mouth.

Tiny looked surprised and then he began to laugh. "You snorted. The Mango Queen snorts when she laughs!"

"Mango Queen? Is that what you call me?"

He looked bewildered, as if he didn't know what to say. Then suddenly, he turned, grabbed her shoulders and brought his lips to hers. If he'd meant it to be a quick smack, he was mistaken, for she wrapped her arms around his neck and kissed him back.

When she released him, he looked shook up. Brianna turned toward the windshield and smiled as butterflies flitted around her stomach.

"I don't know what you're saying half the time, but I'm attracted to you like a bear to honey," Tiny declared after a few moments.

The sun had disappeared and the horizon was as soft as pink cotton candy. In the waning sunlight, Brianna could clearly see the crossroads at the entrance to the park.

"You see, all my life I've been expected to be a certain way. I moved here because I want change. And because of you."

"You came out here because of me?" Tiny's voice sounded faint.

Brianna noted that he had beads of sweat on his forehead.

"Not just you. Also, Kate and Kelly and Amber. However, Tiny, if God speaks to hearts, then he's told me that you're a special guy. I think you are the honey."

"Does that mean that you'll be my Mango Queen?" he asked.

Chapter 5

# Under the Influence

The road to Cottonwood City was quiet as Tiny drove home. He couldn't believe he'd kissed Brianna Davis. He broke out in a sweat thinking about it. *Man, what am I doing? We're as different as diamonds and doughnuts.*

He had met Brianna last year at Kelly and Amber's wedding. It took less than a second that day to decide she was a snobby, big city gal. The woman looked like a beauty queen and behaved like royalty. Held her head high and threw her skinny shoulders back. He figured the orangey dress she wore cost a thousand bucks. Way out of his league.

Right away, he'd dubbed her the Mango Queen. He was surprised by how much he disliked her. After all, he got along with almost everyone. Despite his low opinion of Brianna at the wedding, Tiny had gone out of his way to offer to get her some punch. She had snubbed him.

*God has a sense of humor*, he now thought. Soon, Brianna had stumbled into a gopher hole in the churchyard and he'd rushed to help her. Then, Kate Schulte drafted him into taking her to the emergency room in Bismarck, where it was determined that she had a fractured ankle. Now, months later she had shocked him, shocked everyone, by moving to Schulteville.

He'd had zero hope of being friends with her, yet tonight she sat in his pickup talking some kind of female nonsense to him. There was a God in heaven and He'd heard Tiny's prayers.

Their conversation tonight had been wilder than anything he could imagine. She'd partly moved here because of him. Him. And she snorted when she laughed. Did he really ask her to be his Mango Queen?

Tiny almost drove off the road thinking about it. He was in deep. Deeper than he'd ever been with a woman. Not just any woman. No, he was Evil Knievel jumping the Snake River Canyon. *The snake. The temptation that got Adam and Eve in trouble*, he thought.

Then he noticed a flashing red light following him.

"What now?" he exclaimed, as he steered to the side of the road.

Bill Pickle got out of the squad car. Tiny lowered his window.

"Hey, Bill." He was thankful that the county sheriff was a friend. This stop wouldn't end up like some of those crime shows on television.

"Hey Tiny. You've been driving all over the road and ran a stop sign back there."

"I did?"

Bill held up a flashlight and shined it in Tiny's face. "Have you been drinking?"

"You know I don't drink." Then he laid his head on the steering wheel and muttered. "But I might be DUI-B."

"What's that? Let me see your driver's license."

"Driving under the influence of Brianna," Tiny croaked. Bill gave him a strange look before he walked back to the squad car with his license.

He was back in a few minutes. "You have a perfect driving record, except when you hit that deer last year. I know you haven't been drinking, so what's up? Say, didn't I hear something about you and that San Fran woman that moved here?"

"Yep. That's the source of my problem. I was just on a date with Brianna Davis and she makes me loopy."

"She's a looker," Bill said. "But my advice is don't get too attached. She doesn't look like the type that could make it through a North Dakota winter."

Tiny hadn't considered that.

"I'll let you go with a warning, but if I see any more exhibition driving, I'll give you a ticket," Bill declared as he slapped him on the shoulder.

For the last couple of miles, Tiny creeped along the road below the speed limit, making sure he stayed between the lines. Bill followed him to town, then waved and went back out on the highway.

He was a ball of utter confusion. Rather than going home, he walked around town. He'd been tossing around the idea of buying some exercise equipment. Now he wished he could blow off some steam by lifting weights. He did his best praying when his body was in motion.

# Chapter 6

# Breakfast with Kate

The morning after her date with Tiny, Brianna joined Kate for breakfast in the dining room. Her first week at Kate's place had been so intense that they hadn't even discussed their new business venture. However, this morning Marge and Wayne had left to run errands in Bismarck. With the house to themselves, it was time to broach the subject.

Brianna sat across from Kate at the gleaming Chippendale dining table. Although the moving truck with Brianna's belongings had yet to arrive, she had the forethought to pack her French press coffeepot. It now sat steeping at her elbow as she stirred a bowl of yogurt, blueberries and granola.

Kate was well into a bowl of plain oatmeal. A small glass of prune juice sat properly on the right side of the placemat, while her favorite china teacup was to the left.

"I see you're eating better," Kate sniffed. "Although why you need that ridiculous coffee maker is beyond me." The older woman sat queenly erect, her white hair as fluffy as a Pomeranian, and her yellow bathrobe wrapped tightly around her ample bosom.

Brianna sat erectly as she slowly pressed the plunger on her coffee pot. *She's like a tiger ready for a scrap*, Brianna thought, refusing to take the bait.

"It seems hazy today," she said as she casually looked out the window. "I wonder if the smoke from those fires in the Cascades is drifting this far east? I didn't expect to find fog and smog here."

Kate quaffed down her prune juice and grimaced. However, the challenging look disappeared from her face as Kate-the-teacher appeared. "The smoke won't stay long," she instructed. "Once the wind changes direction and the fires are out, we'll have clear skies again."

Brianna poured her coffee and relished the rich full-bodied flavor before moving to her intended subject. "I'm glad we have time to talk about our plans for the bed and breakfast. I'd really like to have it open for the Christmas season."

She could envision the house restored to its former grandeur. She could see guests arriving to fill all of the rooms. She could smell Marge's breakfast creations and hear the relaxed chatter around this very table. What she wasn't sure about was Kate.

They'd already had the yellow discussion. Kate's propensity for the color was legendary in the county. Before Brianna arranged to move here, they had come to an agreement. The outside of the house and Kate's bedroom would remain yellow. The rest needed a change of color.

It made Brianna uneasy that Kate had been mute on the topic since she'd arrived. Time was flying by and Brianna was ready to dive into redecorating the house. Now she serenely stared at Kate, waiting for her response.

"As far as I'm concerned, everything we discussed when you were here this summer is still in place," Kate answered. "Let's do it! With help from the Good Lord, we'll have success."

Brianna's eyes narrowed. "Getting the house ready is going to take a lot of work."

"I am ready for a challenge," Kate said, holding up her now cold cup of tea to toast the project. "Young lady, you use your skills to update this old house and I'll use my checkbook to pay for the changes. Up to a certain point, of course.”

Wondering where that certain point was, Brianna leaned back in her chair. “Kate, you’re one of the wonders of the world.”

The woman truly was a wonder. At eighty-eight, the prune juice and a handful of vitamins were her only medications. She used a cane to get around, but there was nothing wrong with her brain.

Amber and Kelly had told Brianna that Kate had seemed depressed after her brother died. Now there wasn’t a hint of self-pity about her.

As if reading her thoughts, Kate said, “When my brother died, I didn’t think I could go on. I was a little angry that I kept waking up every morning when the rest of my family was together in heaven.

“How I wanted to wither away,” she said dramatically, causing Brianna to hide a smile behind her coffee mug. “Then Amber needed help with her wedding and you needed a place to stay. You girls gave me purpose. I decided as long as I’m living and breathing, I will do what the Lord puts before me.”

“I hope I have your zest for life when I’m your age,” Brianna responded truthfully.

“There are a couple things we must do,” Kate said, brushing off the compliment. “We must walk through the house and decide what needs updating. Then, we’ll need to research government regulations and draw up legal papers.”

Then to Brianna’s surprise, Kate leaned forward, her eyes shining. “I have a surprise for you! I’ve booked our first guests for the week after next.”

Brianna choked on her coffee and went on a coughing jag. When she could breathe again, she exclaimed, “You what? Why didn’t you say something earlier? We aren’t ready for guests!” *I had better add another description of*

Kate waved off her concern. "Oh, don't worry. The guest is a woman who grew up here. She called to see if she and her sister could tour the house. She always loved it as a child and wondered what it looked like inside.

"I told her we were opening a bed and breakfast and asked if they'd like to spend a complimentary night and give us suggestions."

"In that case, we better go through the house now and decide what must be done immediately." Brianna jumped up to clear the table.

The kitchen had the ambiance she wanted for the rest of the house. The room had original wainscoting on the walls and a long cast iron farm sink surrounded by white cabinets. A modern gas range sat where a cook stove once reigned. She knew that because she'd found the old stove in the storage shed.

A Conestoga hutch, the kind with a built-in place for flour, sat in a nook. A large oak table served as a central island to eat, mix up bread or prepare garden vegetables for the freezer. She especially liked the black and white tile flooring that had been installed just a few years ago. The white Belgium lace curtains were appealing, but not fussy, and there wasn't even a yellow towel to be seen in the kitchen.

It was time to talk about the yellow issue again. "Kate," she said, "Do you see anything different in here than in the rest of the house?"

"Of course. The kitchen has appliances."

"Yes, it does," Brianna conceded. "But also, it isn't *yellow*."

Kate's chin went up. "Yellow is my signature color."

Brianna smiled and spoke calmly, just as she would with a client. "Oh Kate, don't worry. The outside of the house is yellow. You can wear all the yellow you want.

We'll even leave your bedroom yellow."

Pulling Kate along, she went back into the dining room and pointed to the yellow wallpaper that was beginning to peel. Slowly she shook her head. "Look at this. It doesn't represent you at all. We can add spots of yellow in each room, but I believe a more neutral palette will bring out the true grace of the house."

Kate stared at the table and long matching sideboard. Light filtered through the large window and the colored glass at the top made rainbows splash across the walls. "This room is filled with glorious memories."

Brianna walked over to the built-in china hutch that covered one wall. It was full of silver and china. "We should spend some time talking about these beautiful items and then record the information. We could set little cards around telling the stories of some pieces."

She was surprised to see a shimmer of tears in Kate's eyes as she turned away. "That would be a delightful way to show off the heritage of this house. That's why you are one of 'my girls.' 'Twas lonely before you arrived. Who else would care enough to take on a project like this with a cantankerous old woman?"

Brianna impulsively wrapped her arms around Kate and hugged her tight. "We're going to make a great team," she said, as much to herself as to Kate.

She had a lot on her plate. Spiritually, she was growing each day through prayer and Bible study. Emotionally, she was cutting ties with the memory of Kyle Jorgenson and allowing Tiny into the empty space in her heart.

However, questions were edging around her mind. Her parents had practically disappeared from her life when they moved overseas. She had let them know she was moving, but they hadn't responded yet.

At one time, their lives had seemed normal, but now she wondered. As she watched Amber and the McLean family interact, Brianna realized that as she grew up, things hadn't been right. Understanding her family was like putting a puzzle together, except some of the pieces were missing.

# Chapter 7

# The Queen Anne Tour

Brianna and Kate spent several hours touring the house and discussing decorating ideas. Although small, the foyer provided a striking entrance to the house with its mahogany staircase and elegant archway into the parlor. Brianna thought how warm and charming it was compared to the industrial look she'd worked with in the past. A little freshening would make it pop.

Next, they went upstairs. Kate took the stairs one at a time. Brianna followed behind, prepared to catch her if she stumbled.

Once they arrived, Brianna took out her notebook and made a page for each room. Each one was filled with vintage furnishings. She might move things around a bit, but these special pieces were the kind of things that drew guests. She made notes on each page, "Change the wallpaper" or "new drapes."

The closets were impossibly small and packed to the ceiling with hangers of stale, smelling clothes and generations of shoes. Among them, she spied several lovely vintage quilts they could use in the guest rooms.

Two bedrooms shared a Jack and Jill bathroom. They were cozy rather than spacious, but Brianna thought a queen bed would fit in each room.

"This was Ted's room," Kate explained when they entered a French blue chamber. "It was his room until he went into the nursing home. He didn't want yellow in here."

The room held a double bed, highboy chest of drawers and a desk. A wingback chair sat near the window. A stack of his books and Bibles was still piled on the end table. Kate waited for her reaction.

Brianna nodded as she looked around. "The color is a little dated, but the lighting in the room lends itself well to blue. We can leave it much the same. Let's call it Ted's Room."

Kate clapped her hands. "Oh, I'd like that!" Then she reached into the tiny closet for a wooden box, and pulled out a stuffed bear. "Maybe Ted's bear can be a mascot for this room."

Brianna smiled. "You're getting into the theme of things, Kate."

Moving through the shared bathroom, she noted that it would need serious updating. The old-fashioned claw-foot tub and pedestal sink would be pleasant only when the rust and calcium deposits were eliminated. And the wallpaper, ugh. Besides, who knew what kind of problems they might find in the plumbing and electrical?

As she stepped from the bathroom into the room Kate had once occupied, she was enchanted. "I love this room! We must call this Kate's Room."

Kate beamed and clasped her hands in front of her, pleased with Brianna's enthusiasm. "Ted's Room and Kate's Room. I think we have a plan."

Kate had used this room until a few years ago. Rather than being girlish, the furnishings had austere Shaker lines. The centerpiece was a four-poster bed. Brianna ran her hand over the smooth, albeit dusty surfaces. The room was so pleasing that Brianna even liked the veritable garden of tiny yellow roses on the walls.

At the end of the hall, Kate threw open a set of double doors to reveal a room that was almost the width of the house. The focal point was a bay window that brightened the room and had a cozy window seat. A fireplace on one end of the room added a romantic touch.

Then, Brianna focused on the walls and she began to feel queasy. The whole room was decorated with gold striped wallpaper and gold carpeting. She had hoped their first guests might stay in this room, but updating it would take too long.

"Kate, is this wallpaper original to the house?"

"Oh, no. This was Momma and Papa's room. She preferred a soft green. After they were gone, we decided to make it into a guest room. You know, Ted was a pastor and he liked to host visitors. Missionaries and speakers from around the world stayed here at one time or another."

"So you chose the gold colors?"

"Actually it's Mustard Seed Yellow." Kate sounded a bit defensive. "You aren't old enough to remember how popular gold was in the 1970s. We wanted to treat our guests to a really nice place to stay."

*How décor has changed*, Brianna thought. There was no way she could redo this room in a few days. After changes were agreed upon, she'd need to locate paint. And carpeting! Just stripping the wallpaper could take days and the woodwork needed sprucing up.

She sank into a comfy green velvet chair and ottoman near the window. "Was this your mother's or did you add it in the 1970s?" she asked.

"That was Momma's. I couldn't bear to part with her prayer chair. It matched the original color of the walls." Then as an afterthought she added, "This isn't really wallpaper, you know."

"What do you mean?" Brianna strode to a wall and touched it.

"It's paint," Kate explained. "Painting stripes on walls was very trendy at the time."

"It's paint? Why, we could paint over this Mustard Seed Yellow a lot easier than we could pull off wallpaper.

Kate, what do you say we make this room look like it did originally?"

"Momma would like that."

"Good!" Brianna exclaimed. "Let's call this...what was your mother's name?"

"Martha."

"We'll name it Martha's Room in her honor." *Happy, happy, happy,* Brianna thought.

They passed by the hall bathroom. Brianna had already formed a plan to update it so there was no need to look at it again.

The fourth bedroom had served as a sewing room. A treadle sewing machine and a modern electric model were still present. A dressmaker form stood in one corner. Busy wallpaper with flowers and stripes covered the walls.

"It's small, but a single bed would fit in here. We can decorate it with sewing objects and call it the Sewing Room. For now, I might use this for my own sewing projects."

Kate concurred.

Moving back into the hall, Brianna tapped her lips with her forefinger. There was no way they'd get the bathrooms finished in a few days. However, she could transform one bedroom before the first guests arrived.

After another tour along the hallway, they agreed to start work in the big front room. It would be much easier and take less time to paint its long walls than to remove wallpaper from the smaller rooms. Her mind began to spin out ideas. She didn't know how she'd take care of the flooring on such short notice, but she'd try.

As they were about to go downstairs, she stopped by the room with the four-poster bed.

"You seem taken with this room," Kate said. "If you want to move into it, I suspect you could use it for some time before it becomes a guest room."

Originally, Brianna had hoped to make the turret into her nest, but after staying on the third floor for a while, she realized it was impractical. On the other hand, the cozy four-poster room beckoned to her.

"Thanks. I would like to move in here. If we have enough business, perhaps we could turn the turret into a guest room. That would be novel."

After their tour, Kate and Brianna decided to share a pot of tea in the parlor. They were still sitting there when Marge and Wayne arrived home. When Marge dropped the mail on a table, Brianna saw an envelope with her name on it.

The handwriting didn't belong to either of her parents. Frowning, she opened it.

"A birthday card." Then she read the signature and groaned.

"Is your birthday soon, Dear?" asked Marge.

"In a few days."

"We'll need to plan a birthday party," Marge said with a gleam in her eye.

"Is the card from your parents?" Kate asked when she saw Brianna's facial expression.

"No. It's from my Uncle Fab." *Why do I hear from him and not my parents?*

Trying to recover, Brianna changed the subject by brightly asking Wayne, "Would you take me over to your carpentry shop? I'd like to see what kind of wood scraps you have."

"Wood scraps? You've come to the right place," Wayne said agreeably. "Let's go look right now. I need to drop off some supplies anyway."

Brianna tucked the birthday card into her jacket pocket and followed Wayne to the shop. She'd deal with the card later.

Cross Church Carpentry was across the street. When

the church had closed recently, the building had been deeded over to Wayne to use as his shop. It seemed appropriate, since he and Marge had voluntarily cared for the church for years. Besides, his business was outgrowing the old mobile home where it was housed.

He was now shipping handmade pulpits and other furnishings nationwide. In addition, the shop had become the village hub with visitors stopping by for coffee and a chat.

Brianna inhaled the aroma of fresh-cut wood as she came in the door. It ranked right up there with the scent of sweet clover and the fragrance of Marge's yeasty bread coming out of the oven.

"What a wonderful place to work," she said as she looked around the shop that filled the former sanctuary. "It not only smells good, but there is a great sense of peace."

Walking around, she examined the tools he used. A band saw, lathe, drills, vices. Other tools were neatly hung on the walls. He had been disassembling the old wooden church pews, which lay in stacks according to their shapes. She noted he was building at least three kinds of pulpits.

"I had no idea what interesting work you do. We might need your skills when we start remodeling."

Wayne looked at her questioningly.

Brianna sighed. "After touring the house, I thought about the pieces we might want to add to the guest rooms. Headboards, cornices, wall hangings. Perhaps a new window seat. Will you help us?'

"Of course, I'll help. We can all work together."

"I need advice, too. Where can I get paint and carpeting? This week."

He chuckled, not quite believing her timeline.

The thought of guests arriving so soon was exciting, although she'd have to put in many hours to be ready. Still, she didn't mind. Redecorating a room was a lot easier than dealing with her parents and Uncle Fab.

Chapter 8

# The Birthday Party

Although Brianna was busy, her thoughts often strayed to her parents. She'd tried to contact them several times to say she'd moved. They hadn't responded, which was unusual, even for her family. She still had the same phone number and email address, and Uncle Fab had reached her, so what was the problem?

Wayne had helped her move the furniture from the front bedroom into the wide hallway. Together they decided what else needed to be done. Tear up the carpet and haul it out. Clear the closet and paint it. Put two coats of paint on the walls, one on the ceiling. Sand and varnish the dark woodwork on the windows and doors.

She had also agreed to help Amber decorate her new office in Cottonwood City. She was set to open Gates Insurance North in a few weeks. Of course, no decorating project ever took place without a shopping trip, so tomorrow they planned a run to Bismarck.

*It's good that I can still sit at my computer and work for Jontel,* she thought wryly. *Otherwise, I'd drop from fatigue from all of this manual labor.*

Brianna borrowed a crowbar from Wayne and began prying up the carpet in the front bedroom. What was underneath astounded her. Smooth wide boards stained dark to match the woodwork.

She scrambled to her feet and called to Kate, who peered up at her from the first floor.

"Did Martha's Room have carpeting or hardwood flooring?" she queried.

"Hardwood. There was no such thing as wall-to-wall carpeting back then. 'Twas covered with a lovely Turkish rug. 'Tis still in the attic."

Brianna turned and bounded up the stairs to the third floor and pushed open the door to the storage room. Searching in the dark, she found the pull string to the light switch and an exquisite paradise of antiques appeared.

Seeing all the wonderful finds, she felt like a kid on Christmas morning. It took a few minutes to locate the rug on the far edge of the room. She cleared some space and rolled it. *Exquisite. If moths haven't eaten into it, the rug can go back in Martha's Room.*

From a distance, she heard Kate calling her. "Brianna, you have company!" Just then, the hall clock chimed six times.

*Oh no*, she thought. *Tiny was coming to pick me up.* The day had disappeared like a mile marker on the highway. She turned off the light and shut the door. Bounding down both flights of stairs, she skidded into the foyer.

Tiny, Amber and Kelly stood beaming at her. "Happy birthday!" they exclaimed.

Amber's eyes got big when she saw her disheveled friend. Brianna was aware that her jeans were gray with dirt and her shirt was only half tucked in. Her hair was pulled back in a ponytail and any makeup she might have worn had been washed away by sweat.

Her mouth dropped open. "Hi. Tiny. I got caught up in my project and lost track of time," she started to explain. "Wait, why are you here, Amber and Kelly?

Amber's laughter rang like a joyous bell. "We're going out for buffalo burgers to help you celebrate your birthday. There's also a birthday cake waiting at our place."

*No one seems to understand my dietary rules, Bri-anna thought.*

However, Amber poked a hole in her list of rules. "You'll love buffalo. It's lean. Organically grown."

"Yeah, and it's good, too," Tiny added.

Amber glowed. "I'm so excited. My new Jeep arrived today, so I'm driving."

Brianna's heart melted. A few months ago, Amber had been critically injured in an accident. But for God's grace and healing power, she wouldn't be standing here right now.

"I'm so glad you have a new set of wheels," Brianna said. "But, back up a moment. How did any of you know it's my birthday tomorrow?"

She watched as Amber, Kelly and Tiny's eyes strayed to Kate and Marge. The two women stood piously side by side, their hands folded in front of them.

Brianna smiled and shook her head. "You two!"

Marge shrugged her shoulders and smiled. "Go get showered and changed. I'll bring out some appetizers for your guests."

"You guys are the best friends ever!" Brianna said, and then turned abruptly toward the stairs, hoping no one saw her tears.

She only made it halfway up the steps before she heard Tiny ask, "Why's she crying?"

Before long, Brianna swept down the stairs dressed in black pants and a glittery top under a turquoise silk bomber jacket. She had pulled her heavy dark hair back to reveal dangly silver earrings. With her makeup perfectly in place, she was her normal poised self. Her fingernails were the only sign of labor. She had filed them back to her fingertips.

Tiny's eyes glazed over as he stood up. "Wow."

"You look gorgeous, Birthday Girl!" Amber jumped in. "Let's go. I can't wait to give you a ride."

"Yeah, just make sure she isn't on the phone when she's at the wheel," Kelly teased.

"Hey, I wasn't talking on the phone when the accident happened," Amber answered piously. "I was looking for it in my purse."

With thanks for the refreshments, the party of four left.

Eating buffalo burgers with friends at a rustic restaurant with a view of the rolling Dakota plains was far different than her last birthday celebration. Then, she'd dined at an elegant restaurant atop a San Francisco skyscraper with Jontel and some of his friends. They had ordered artichoke and black truffle soup and pan-seared calamari from a condescending waiter. Tonight, the waitress wore tennis shoes and kept a notepad in the back pocket of her jeans.

After dinner, the party adjourned to the parsonage. Brianna glided into a chair at the dining room table. She noted that Kelly had cleared off his textbooks and Amber had set the table with the couple's Fiesta dessert dishes. Tiny and Kelly sat on each side of her. Brianna's nose started itching even before she saw Mildred the cat flicking her tail from the staircase.

All of their eyes were on the door to the kitchen. When Amber walked in with the birthday cake, Brianna broke out laughing.

"A sunflower cake!" she exclaimed. The eye-catching confection was decorated with yellow petals made of Peeps. The middle was filled with chocolate chips representing sun seeds.

"I've got a talented wife," Kelly bragged. "And she knows how much I like Peeps."

"Who doesn't like Peeps?" Tiny said with a big smile on his face.

"We need to take a picture before we dive into this," Brianna said as she reached for her phone. "Glad I've got a good camera on my phone." They took turns snapping pics of each other and the cake.

She couldn't help but think of how sunflowers had helped draw her to this rural life. It seemed appropriate that her birthday was in the season when sunflowers were being harvested.

Before they settled into eating the cake, Kelly offered a prayer for her. "Brianna, this prayer is a paraphrase of some verses from Isaiah 61." He bent his head and the others followed.

"Lord, I pray for a year of favor for our friend, Brianna. I pray that you will give her beauty for the ashes of the longtime grief she has had. Give her the oil of joy and clothe her in a garment of praise. Pour out abundant blessings of wisdom, joy and peace on her, and bless the work of her hands. In the precious name of our Lord Jesus. Amen."

Brianna stared at her old friend, twin brother of her first love, Kyle. They had been through the valley of the shadow of death together, but now they were on the other side.

"Kelly, did you know that scripture has become very important to me?"

Kelly shook his head and smiled. "No. I was thinking of how special it is to have you living here and Isaiah 61 came to mind. Be blessed by it."

They raised their water glasses in a toast.

"To Brianna. May your life be filled with sunflowers," Amber said.

"May your life be filled with treasures," Kelly added, as they clinked their glasses together.

Tiny began to fidget. "Speaking of treasures, I have a gift for you, out in the pickup."

A minute later, he returned with a gift bag.

Brianna's eyes lit up expectantly as she peeked inside. "Mangoes?"

Tiny studied the table. "They remind me of you," he said sheepishly.

"Oh yes, I heard you call me the Mango Queen." At first that annoyed her, but now his sweet admission made her smile.

"There's something else at the bottom," Tiny said.

Brianna dug through the fruit to a little box. Inside was a pendant the same color as a mango. A note scrawled in Tiny's handwriting stated, *"In India, the mango is considered to be a royal fruit. So I hope it's okay to call you the Mango Queen."*

"That's very thoughtful," she conceded.

"Aw, I just picked it up at the drugstore. Read the card."

The front had a photo of a fruit bowl. Inside the card read, "You did not choose me, but I chose you and appointed you, so that you might go and bear fruit that will last, and so that whatever you ask in my name the Father will give you." John 15:16.

Brianna looked at Tiny and slowly shook her head. "This may be the most thoughtful gift I've ever received." Then, she threw her arms around him.

It felt like she'd escaped from a burning disaster area to a place where hope sprang up like water from a fountain.

Chapter 9

# Brianna Meets Jolina

**B**rianna woke up to see rays of sun highlighting a line on her new wooden plaque. On a whim, she'd designed the plaque when she had an idea for decorating a piece of wood. The paint was hardly dry when she had hung it, replacing the old battered one.

"To proclaim the year of the Lord's favor—."

Every day, the verses on the plaque became more relevant to her. She hadn't even thought about this particular phrase before. Now, with a beam of light shining on it, Brianna thought of what a blessing a year of the Lord's favor could hold.

She snuggled into her bed immersed in happiness and counted her blessings. A birthday party with friends last evening. She was living in a house filled with an architectural ambiance that fed her interest in design. Kate, Marge and Wayne functioned like devoted parents, offering a warmth she hadn't known as a child.

She wondered if it was weird to still need parents. *Maybe I'm regressing. I'll have to ask Amber if she still needs her mom. But, I already know what she'll say. Amber treasures her mother.*

The word "treasure" reminded her again of the birthday party. The merry affair had satisfied her craving for friendship. And more. When Tiny drove her home, he'd pulled over before they arrived at the house so they wouldn't be interrupted by a blinking porch light. It seemed that Tiny was getting over his fear of kissing her.

Now as the beam of sunlight moved, the stem of the sunflower she had painted on the plaque glowed in the early morning light. It reminded her that she needed to keep the stem of her faith rooted in her relationship with God.

Her thoughts drifted to the first time she saw a field of sunflowers, their golden heads all facing toward the rising sun. Their rough petals, leaves and stems were rustic, but their sunny faces always brought a smile. They were a symbol of peace, hope and happiness.

Amber had given Brianna the rest of the sunflower birthday cake to take home. However, it was more than her housemates could eat. Besides, Marge planned to make a low-calorie birthday dessert for her.

Tiny hadn't said much about his mother, although Brianna understood the woman had some mental health issues. All she really knew was that they lived together in a doublewide near Your Friendly Co-op.

*Wouldn't it be fun to drop off some cake at Tiny's house? What a perfect excuse to meet his mother*, she thought. *I could stop there before Amber and I leave for Bismarck.*

An hour later, with the confectionary sunflower on the seat next to her and a shopping list in her purse, Brianna reached the edge of Cottonwood City. As she slowed to turn off the highway, she spied Tiny driving a tow truck in the opposite direction. She raised her forefinger from the steering wheel in greeting like she'd seen others do.

*So different than the one-fingered salutes given in the city*, she thought.

She eased the Miata into the long driveway to the mobile home and put it in park. Tiny's home was about what she expected. An aging, beige doublewide with aluminum-framed windows.

Stepping out of the car, she adjusted her dark glasses and smoothed her clothes. After days of wearing grungy garments for pulling up carpet and scraping paint, it felt good to put on a business outfit. The three-quarter length light wool coatdress was warm enough for the chilly fall weather, but light enough to wear all day. She had paired it with skinny pants and flat shoes. The necklace from Tiny was around her neck.

After removing the cake from the car, Brianna took a deep breath and said a prayer. She really wanted to make a good impression on Tiny's mother. Stepping onto the wood porch, she saw that the doorbell was broken, so she knocked lightly on the front door.

Listening, she realized a television program was blaring inside, so she rapped harder. She smiled in anticipation of Tiny's mother opening the door in delighted surprise. She'd say, "Hi, Mrs. Winger. I'm Brianna Davis, Tiny's friend. I thought maybe you and Tiny would like a couple pieces of my birthday—."

Before completing her thought, the door flew open and a chill came over Brianna.

The woman who answered couldn't possibly be Tiny's mother. For one thing, no one that small could produce a big boy like Tiny. Before her stood a disheveled little woman with the meanest eyes she'd ever seen and a cigarette dangling from her mouth. She was dressed in a short housecoat, white anklets and slippers.

Brianna took off her sunglasses and the two sized each other up.

"Get off my property!" the woman croaked in a threatening voice. "Or I'll get the broom and sweep you out of here."

"Mrs. Winger?" Brianna asked tentatively.

"You got a hearing problem? I said get out of here!"

"Listen, I'm not a salesperson, I'm Tiny's friend."

"Get out! Get out! Get out!" the woman shouted.

Brianna's mouth dropped open and she couldn't move. If this was Tiny's mother, maybe Brianna didn't know him as well as she thought. Finally, she took a couple steps backward.

"Whatcha got there?" The woman had taken the cigarette out of her mouth and was staring at the cake.

"I brought some cake for you and Tiny. But, that's okay. I'll leave," Brianna stammered.

"Gimme the cake."

Brianna gulped. She'd never met anyone this scary, even on the streets of San Francisco. "You are Tiny's mother?" she asked, hoping to hear she was at the wrong address.

When the woman nodded curtly, Brianna handed over the cake. It looked so perky on one of Kate's kitchen plates.

The woman held the cake close to her face and peered at it. Brianna suddenly realized how strange the yellow and black baked goods might look.

"It's a sunflower cake, Mrs. Winger."

"This piece of crap is no sunflower," Jolina said, raising the plate over her head.

"No! Don't throw it! Give it back. Give it back!"

However, it was too late. Jolina threw the cake at Brianna. The sticky frosting glued yellow Peeps to the front of her wool coatdress. The plate crashed to the porch and shattered.

"Why did you do that?" she cried, swiping at the glutinous mess that had splattered onto her face.

"Get off my property or I'll call the cops. And don't even think about being friends with my son. You aren't his type."

Brianna looked at Kate's broken plate and then up at the woman.

"You're rude and you don't scare me," she said as calmly as possible.

She turned and walked to her car and slid in. Safe inside, Brianna realized her hands were shaking. Taking a deep breath, she pasted a smile on her face and managed to put the car in gear. She backed down the driveway and drove away before bursting into tears.

While she'd been proud to wave at Tiny earlier, she now hoped no one would recognize her. She drove the few blocks to Amber's new office. The Jeep was parked out front and Brianna pulled in behind it. After wiping her eyes with a tissue and blotting more gunk from her face, she looked around. It was early and traffic on Main Street was light as she bolted from the car into the building.

Amber took one look at her and burst out laughing.

"What happened to you? It looks like you had a run-in with a herd of Peeps."

Brianna leaned against the wall, willing her tears to dry up.

"Worse than that. What do you know about Tiny's mother?"

Chapter 10

# Jolina, Jolina

From the safety of her recliner, Jolina Winger sat in front of the television watching reruns and waiting for her regular game show to come on. Every few moments, she turned to look out the front window of the mobile home.

She peered past the clump of leafless chokecherry trees and the standard galvanized metal mailbox at the end of the long driveway. Your Friendly Co-op stood a block away. She had positioned her chair for a birds-eye view of the shop where her only son, Tiny, spent most of his time.

Things had changed for the better when J.D. died, she thought. She had no remorse over her husband's early death, only relief from the fear and violence of living with him. The moment he died, she knew whatever came next had to be better. And it was. The state paid her a little income and Tiny took care of her.

Jolina liked being alone. Marriage to that brute, J.D, had forced her to live in isolation. Besides, people shunned her for being different. No problem. She shunned them, too.

She shook another cigarette from the pack beside her chair and lit it from one burning in an ashtray overflowing with butts. After her husband's death, Jolina had simply detached herself from the world. She'd moved out of the master bedroom at the front of the doublewide trailer and let Tiny have the larger space. She now occupied the two rooms at the back of the house, using one as her bedroom and one for crafts. She could putter there, and she could think, and no one bothered her.

Sometimes she felt like a tree that survived wind and drought, and now stood a twisted reflection of what it could have been. But, usually she was too busy to think about the past.

When she wasn't in her craft room, Jolina spent her days spying on the Co-op. She knew who got gas and who needed a tire changed. She knew when Tiny was at the shop, and when he wasn't. A few minutes ago, he'd driven off in the tow truck.

Now to her surprise, a little red sports car pulled slowly into her driveway. Why, only a few months ago she'd been surprised to see that Schulte woman's big black car pull up. Too much traffic all the time, she thought.

She sank into the memory of the day Tiny had gone to the wedding. Most everybody in town must have been there, too. Things had been slow at the Co-op. Nothing had stirred until midafternoon, when Kate Schulte's Cadillac had pulled up to the gas pump. The next thing she knew, the Cadillac rolled up Jolina's driveway, as this little spit of a car did now. She remembered being surprised when Tiny got out of the driver's door. Just thinking about it now made her roll her hands in agitation as she replayed the scene.

She remembered how Tiny had burst through the front door carrying a stack of paper plates wrapped in cellophane. He'd rushed to the fridge and slid the stack onto the empty shelf.

"Ma, I have to go to Bismarck. Rusty said he'll close the shop at six o'clock."

She had tried to ignore him, but he strode over and turned off the television.

"Ma, the wedding was great. Pastor Kelly and Amber Rose are officially married. Imagine that!" She'd have to use her imagination. She'd never met these people.

Tiny loosened his tie and threw it on a chair. "Hey, we have sandwiches and salads and wedding cake to eat. I won't have to cook for a couple days!"

Jolina had taken a drag on her cigarette, and then reached for the remote and turned the television back on. Tiny's shoulders sagged a bit and then he'd grabbed the remote from her and turned the volume down.

"Ma, the strangest thing happened. The bridesmaid hurt her ankle bad. She's from San Francisco. She wore this skinny dress and highfalutin shoes. Down she went!" Tiny slapped his hands together, showing how quickly the accident had happened.

He'd rambled on about driving the bridesmaid to the emergency room in Bismarck and how Kate Schulte had loaned her car for the trip. Jolina remained mute, letting his words bounce back to him as though unheard. He'd finally gave up and puffed down the hall to his room. A couple minutes later he returned wearing a t-shirt and jeans.

Walking to the door without looking back, he said, "Her name is Brianna Davis."

Now, outside the window, Jolina saw a tall, dark-haired woman unfold from the small car. When she heard a polite knock on the door, she stubbed out her cigarette and turned up the volume on the television.

She wasn't stupid. Lately, Tiny had been acting strange. Lost some weight. Dressed up to go out for the evening. He'd even cleaned up his pickup. The *Cottonwood Times* had carried a story about a Brianna Davis moving to Schulteville. If this Davis woman thought she could upset Jolina's life, she had another think coming.

The knocking on the door grew louder. Jolina lit another smoke and blew out the match. Whoever it was needed a good kick in the pants. She got up and flung open the door.

The woman before her was a young thing. Such a pretty face and fancy clothes. She held out something that looked like a frosted honeybee and began to yammer on, introducing herself as Brianna Davis.

Something exploded in Jolina. Who did this hotshot from San Francisco think she was, knocking on Jolina's door? Acting all uppity. Offering her a crappy slice of cake. Taking away her only son.

It was all Jolina could do to keep from lunging at the woman. Instead, she took the offered plate and studied it. Then, she lifted it high and pitched it with both hands. The shocked look on the woman's face was priceless. Jolina almost laughed aloud.

Leaving the trollop covered in cake, Jolina stepped into the house and slammed the door so hard the walls shook. She turned the lock and leaned against the door. She hadn't felt this good since J.D. died.

Walking past the blaring television, she went to her craft room at the back of the house. She looked around the room at all the ragdolls she'd made. They ranged in size from a three-foot softie that sat on the dresser to Sassy, who was small enough to sit in the palm of her hand.

The small room held a chest of drawers filled with yarn, lace and other sewing notions. One whole drawer had old pantyhose collected from here and there that she used to stuff her dolls. Bolts of fabric sorted by color were stacked on shelves. Her rocking chair was positioned by the window that looked toward Main Street. The table in the middle of the room held her sewing machine, an older but reliable model. The table was marred from the cutting wheels and scissors used to form her dolls and their clothes.

Designing your friends had its advantages. Jolina's dolls always understood her, always took her side.

"Well, Sassy, Tiny has a girlfriend. What do you think of that?" Jolina picked the doll up and held her at eye level.

"What's that? You don't think any good can come of this? Me either." She held the doll close to her ear. "Yes, I agree, she should go back to San Francisco where she belongs," Jolina said as she stroked the doll's strawberry blonde yarn hair.

"Soon, Sassy. She should go back soon."

Jolina put the doll down and went to the table where fabric was cut for yet another doll. She collected the pieces and sat down at her sewing machine, but she was too distracted to begin stitching the doll together.

"Don't he know his place yet? He has a good life running the Co-op and taking care of his mother," she muttered. She pushed away from the sewing machine and lit a cigarette. Standing by the window, she drew deeply and blew smoke from her nose.

"Yes, my friends, we must watch Tiny carefully," Jolina explained to her friends. Turning, she picked up a dark-haired dolly and began pushing pins into its neck. Smiling, she dropped it into a dresser drawer and slammed it shut.

With that, she stubbed out the cigarette and sat down to begin working on her next doll.

# Chapter 11

# Stress Therapy

Brianna cried as she spit out an angry account of her visit with Tiny's mother. Now, she sat wrapped in Amber's jacket in the back room of Gates Insurance North as Amber skillfully blotted Peeps and chocolate chips from her coatdress.

"Jolina has a good arm. You could bring charges against her," Amber said with a straight face. "Assault by cake."

"Amber?" Brianna wondered if her friend was serious.

"I doubt if the charges would stick. Pardon the pun."

That brought a weak smile to Brianna's lips. "You know, you're a good friend. I need some humor to bring down my hysteria."

"I honed my skills while herding four rowdy brothers." Amber held up the outfit. "I think this is good enough to wear when we go across the street to the hardware store. But, before we drive to Bismarck, let's detour over to Schulteville and you can put on a fresh outfit."

Brianna slipped on the dress. "I knew Tiny came from a troubled background, but I thought those problems were in the past. The woman I met today is mentally unhinged. How does Tiny handle it?"

Amber shook her head, her curly blonde hair bouncing with the movement. "That's something to ask him. He was ahead of me in school and then I moved away. I didn't really get to know him until Kelly and I began dating. He's been a real friend to Kelly, who by the way says Tiny is a diamond in the rough."

"Good description." Brianna could feel the tension leaving her neck and back. "Kelly needed a friend when he moved here. Sounds like Tiny needed a buddy even more."

"You know, God has a wonderful plan for your life. Don't let this morning's mishap discourage you." Amber's voice soothed.

"It's too soon to know how I feel about this new twist," Brianna replied. "It's like I was on a nice walk in a park and now find myself in the middle of a wildlife sanctuary." For now, it was time to pull herself together. They had a day of shopping ahead of them.

Happily, Brianna and Amber found paint at the local hardware store for both of their projects. The owner helped them lug the gallons of paint back to the insurance office and Brianna's car. A light caramel for Amber's lobby and bayberry green for Martha's Room.

Before driving to Bismarck, they stopped at Schulteville so Brianna could drop off the paint and change clothes. Afterward, as they cruised out of town, Brianna spied the mail truck. They pulled over and she rifled through the mailbox and pulled out an envelope.

"Look, a nice fat letter from Helena," she exclaimed once she was back in the Jeep. "I haven't heard from my parents for a while, so it's nice to get a birthday card. After this morning, I won't ever complain about them again."

As they hummed along Highway 83, Brianna tore open the envelope and drew out an exquisite hand-drawn card. "Look, this is a perfect example of my mother's artwork and the high standard she sets," Brianna said as she settled back to read the letter.

"I can't believe this," she cried moments later. "So much for having good feelings about my parents!"

"What's wrong?" Amber asked.

"Helena came back from England and left my dad there. She says she didn't like the gloomy weather. The arts community in Southern California needed her." Brianna tapped her lip with her forefinger. "Amber, when I didn't hear from them, I thought they were upset with me, but it had nothing to do with me."

"That's a good thing."

Brianna read the rest of the letter. "Apparently, whoever bought our old house reneged on the contract. Helena is having some work done on it before she moves back in. Right now, she's staying with Uncle Fab."

Amber looked puzzled. "Who's he?"

Brianna groaned. "He's my mother's brother. Something of a gadabout. He and Helena love attending fancy white-tie affairs. Dad hates them. Helena will like being back at our house in Huntington Beach." Her voice trailed off. "What about Dad? Does this mean my parents are separating or will he follow her back?"

Amber remained silent and kept her eyes on the road.

Brianna picked up a photo that had been in the envelope and examined it closely. "This is Mom in an evening gown with Uncle Fab. It's a recent photo."

Amber peeked at the photo. "Fancy! What is your uncle's real name?"

"His name is Fabian Demetri Mond. He coined the name Uncle Fab himself." Brianna slumped down in her seat. *I have mixed feelings about Uncle Fab. Very mixed.*

"Do I detect that you don't think Uncle Fab is so fabulous?"

"That's a good question." How could Amber understand the misery in her childhood? She had seen the farmhouse where Amber grew up. It wasn't as elegant as her homes had been, however their family was the salt of the earth type. Still, Amber was a friend, and weren't pastor's wives supposed to be understanding?

"The truth is every miserable childhood memory I have includes Uncle Fab. No matter where we moved, he was usually around for holidays and sometimes stayed for weeks."

Amber gave her a rueful look, but didn't comment.

Brianna began reading the letter in a throaty voice, mimicking her mother. "Brianna, dear, I do hope you are surviving out there in that cultural wasteland. My deepest love and devotion to my darling daughter on your twenty-third birthday."

She paused for a moment. "Do you notice anything unusual about this?"

"She said you are twenty-three. Aren't you the same age as Kelly and me?"

"Yes, I am. This is pure Helena. She doesn't want her daughter to catch up to her in age!"

Amber wrapped a finger around a strand of hair. "I'm seeing a different side of your life. I always assumed your background was similar to Kelly's, but looks are deceiving, aren't they?"

Brianna thought back. She'd been to the Jorgenson home many times when she was in high school. Kelly and Kyle's home was always relaxed and welcoming. At her house, either a cocktail party was being planned or the remains of one cluttered every room.

As they drove into Bismarck, Amber said, "You've had a lot thrown at you today, literally. It might be a little late in the season for my favorite stress reliever, a giant-size root beer float. So, I'd like to treat you to a birthday lunch at Peacock Alley. That will revive us. Then we can shop 'til we drop."

"That's the worst suggestion you've had since you picked up mint chocolate chip ice cream when I was staying with you last spring," Brianna said brightly. "Let's do it."

They'd beat the lunch crowd by a few minutes and pulled into a parking spot on Fifth Street near the restaurant's door.

"Kelly and I go here for special occasions," Amber explained. "I love the history of the building. Believe it or not, it's been the go-to place for everyone from presidents to mobsters."

Once inside, Brianna gawked at the interior of the historic restaurant. The dark wood paneling gleamed and the chandeliers gave off an elegant ambiance. "This is inspiring," she commented as she gazed at the décor.

When a waitress stopped by with menus, Brianna perused the salad listings. Then her eyes strayed to the sandwiches. "Look, they have a sandwich called The California and it's got some of my favorite ingredients."

Before she could change her mind, Amber had pointed out the sandwich to the server and said, "We'll each have a half sandwich, a cup of beer-cheese soup, and gelato for dessert."

Brianna didn't have the strength to protest, although she wondered how soup made with cheese and beer would taste, and gelato was not on her list of healthy food.

They talked about the morning's events through most of the lunch. When they were finished, Brianna sighed happily. "I hate to admit I had misgivings about the soup, but it was delicious. Maybe there's something to eating carbs while you talk about your problems. Thank you."

Amber reached across the table and took both of her hands. Brianna felt a tingle go up her arms and she looked into Amber's eyes, which now were filled with love.

"I can tell you with some authority that our heavenly Father sees this as a bump in the road. He is more than able and more than willing to help you deal with Tiny's mother and your parents."

Brianna sat with her hands locked with Amber's for several moments. She remembered the car accident Amber had only a few months earlier. No one knew if she'd survive and Brianna had immediately flown to North Dakota to help. When Amber had awakened, she was healed and her personality had changed, too. She was still energetic, but seemed more tranquil.

"I believe you," Brianna said quietly.

"When you pray about this, give it into God's hands and don't take it back. Give faith a road test and see how it works."

Brianna agreed with the advice. "I need to talk this out with Tiny. As far as my parents go, I'll wait until I'm calmer to deal with them."

"Yes." Amber was nodding, her golden ringlets bouncing again. "Let it settle a bit and pray about it before contacting them. We'll be praying, too."

"Oh Amber, you must be the best pastor's wife. Everything about you says, 'Don't worry, God is in control.' You're so wise."

Amber squeezed Brianna's hand again. "No one likes trials, but no matter what we face, eventually we will see something beautiful rise out of the ashes."

"Beauty for ashes. That's in Isaiah 61. Right now it seems like it was written just for me."

"You're getting to know the Bible." Amber noted, "You'll find it often reads like a letter just to you. Now, let's go do some shopping therapy."

By the time the two friends left for home that afternoon, they'd purchased almost everything needed for Amber's office. They'd ordered a desk, cabinets, and a long credenza that would serve as a coffee bar in the lobby.

The Jeep was stuffed with two chairs and decorative pieces for the walls. Plus, Brianna had found creamy white bedding for the bed and breakfast.

Most importantly, after a morning where the bottom had fallen out of her world, Brianna now felt like she was standing on solid ground once again. She just didn't know if she'd be standing there with Tiny.

# Chapter 12

# Tiny Oozes Hope

Tiny knew something was wrong the moment he saw the crumbs of Brianna's sunflower cake and the shattered glass splattered across the front porch.

"Ma!" he called as he tried to open the door and found it locked. "Ma, let me in." There was no answer except the sound of the Second Cavalry coming to someone's rescue on a television rerun.

He stepped off the porch and strode to the side door, which was unlocked. "Ma? Where are you?" He found her sitting in her craft room putting the final stitches on a new rag doll.

"What's with the mess on the front porch?" When she didn't answer, he pulled the doll from her and knelt down to look into her eyes. More calmly, he said, "Tell me."

"A saleswoman in a little sports car tried to sell me some cake. I took care of her."

"What did she look like?"

Jolina began rolling her hands as if she was doing patty cake. It was a sign of agitation.

"She's not for you!" She spit out the words. "I chased her away."

*Brianna. She must have tried to deliver some birthday cake.* He could only imagine the confrontation that had taken place. A bad feeling spread through his body all the way to the toes of his white socks. Why had he even hoped for a future with a woman like Brianna?

"Ma, did you hurt her?" he demanded in a voice that sounded like a frog's croak. Hope oozed from his heart like honey from an overturned jar.

A broad smile brightened Jolina's face and exposed her yellowed teeth. "Oh no. I just had a little fun with her."

"You shouldn't have done that. She's my friend. Or she was." Tiny sighed heavily. "You had no right."

"She was on my property without permission." Jolina held her head high in defiance.

"Ma, we've been over this. Our property. The house has been in my name since I turned twenty-one. You have no right to treat my friends badly."

Jolina turned her head, averting her eyes.

"Have you been taking your medicine?"

*Of course not*, he thought as he got up and went to the kitchen. Each Sunday he measured out her pills for the coming week. That way he could tell if she was taking her medication. She'd missed three days. He took her daily dose back to the craft room along with a glass of water and watched her down the pills.

"I'm going to try to repair the damage you've done. You better hope it isn't too late." He started out of the room and then stopped. "You can clean up the mess on the porch and cook your own supper."

At first, Tiny planned to drive to Schulteville and talk to Brianna, but soon realized he couldn't face her. No woman, and especially Brianna Davis, could overlook whatever had happened today. It was a stretch to believe they were meant to be together. She was diamonds and he was doughnuts.

Next, he considered talking to his friend Kelly. However, he didn't think he could face him, either. Kelly came from a nice, normal family. His father hadn't drunk himself to death, and his mother hadn't been declared incompetent by the courts. How could he understand?

Instead, he went to the diner and ordered the Massive, a double-patty burger loaded with cheese and bacon, plus a fried chicken dinner, and a doughnut for dessert.

"Fell off the wagon, huh?" the waitress asked. Charlotte grew up next door to the Wingers and married a local farmer. She liked to mind his business in a sisterly way.

"And a chocolate malt," he added, not daring to look at her.

"No can do."

Tiny raised his eyes, puzzled.

"We're out of Massive Burgers. How about you just order the grilled chicken?" Charlotte suggested, and then muttered under her breath, "And skip the malt."

"What do you mean, out of Massives? Everybody at that table is chowing down on one."

"None of them have worked so hard at losing weight," she said firmly. "If you want your diet to crash and burn, you'll have to visit the restaurant in Washburn. I won't be a part of you gaining all those pounds back."

Tiny's shoulders slumped. "All right. Just the chicken dinner and a pine float."

"Got it." She smiled as she sashayed away with the order, returning soon with a glass of water with a toothpick in it. "You'll thank me some day."

Later, Tiny cruised around town. The sun went down early this time of year, or he'd go fishing. He drove down the highway east of town until he spied an approach and pulled off the road. The western sky looked like someone had slapped it with orange and purple paint.

Venus was already shining in the western sky, while the moon rose in the east. A guy could see a million stars on a night like this. What Tiny couldn't see was why God would tease him with someone like Brianna and then smash his hopes.

In his head, he knew his mother couldn't help it. More than anyone, he knew what had sent her over the edge.

As a child, he'd watched from behind a piece of furniture more than once as his father beat her. Still, the worst of it had been the way the old man had played her, making promises and breaking them.

He clearly remembered when she'd asked for money to buy groceries. His father had said sure she could have money, and slapped a five-dollar bill in her hand. When he came home from work the next evening, he'd expected steak and potatoes, but she'd only been able to afford bread and milk. That was a bad night.

A couple times, she'd gotten a job, but he wouldn't let her leave the house. When she did, he'd accuse her of all kinds of things.

Through all those years, he'd often gone to school tired from listening to their all night fights. Because there was so little money, he wore shabby clothes and shoes. Winters were really tough, because he usually didn't have a warm jacket, mittens or boots.

His mother had done her best, but as the years went by, she'd withdrawn and rarely spoke. When his father died, she almost seemed relieved.

A rap on the window of his pickup startled Tiny. The sheriff's car had pulled up and Bill Pickle peered at him through the glass.

Tiny lowered the window.

"Woman problems again?" Bill asked.

"More than that," Tiny groaned.

Bill climbed into the passenger seat. "It's going to be a slow night for patrolling, so I've got a little time. What gives?"

"In my head, I know my mother has problems," Tiny explained. "But in my gut—," he didn't know how to finish.

"What did she do this time?"

"Threw a plate of food at Brianna Davis."

"No kidding." A smirk crossed Bill's face.

"Don't laugh, Bill. There's no way I can face Brianna again. I didn't tell her anything about Ma's sickness, so the outburst must have been a total surprise."

"Did this San Fran woman dump you?"

"Well, no."

"Have you even talked to her?"

"No. It's over. She was way out of my league from the beginning. Today only proved it."

"Now, wait a minute," Bill said. "Let's talk about Jolina. Has she been taking her meds?" Along with the social services staff, Bill was one of the few people in town who knew details about his mother's struggle.

"I guess not. She's been getting strange again. I don't always notice right away."

"How long has it been since she was last committed to the hospital?"

Tiny looked up at the bill of his cap, thinking. "Three years."

"Well, then she's about due for a tune-up. She probably needs an evaluation and a look at her medications. That's helped before. You had better get social services involved. Call Sarah as soon as possible. I'll drive her to the State Hospital when the paperwork is ready."

"Thanks, Bill. I shouldn't have let it come to this, but it's about all I can do to keep up with the household stuff. I don't mind, you know. She can't help it."

The sheriff patted the younger man on the shoulder.

"It's just that, well, I'd kind of like to have my own life, too."

"You deserve that. You also deserve a chance with this San Fran woman. Why don't you give her a call? Talk to her about your mother and admit you should have warned her."

"I planned to tell her, but we always ended up, er, talking about other things when we went out." Tiny smiled for the first time.

Bill chuckled and reached for the door handle. "By the way, you were looking at that office space in the Taylor Building. I'm handling the leases on the building for the Taylor family. What are you thinking about doing with it?"

"Oh, that." His idea to open a gym seemed remote now. "I thought about installing some gym equipment. Mostly, I need a space to exercise this winter. I thought maybe other people in town would like to use it, too."

"That's a great idea," Bill said. "And I'm pretty sure the family would make the rent reasonable. Let me know when you want to walk through it."

"Sure thing. First, I better take care of matters at home."

"You bet." Bill slid out of the pickup. "And Tiny, don't let that special woman get away."

# Chapter 13

# Old Rug in the Attic

**W**hen Brianna arrived home from the excursion to Bismarck, there were no messages from Tiny. He didn't call the next day, either. *Maybe Jolina cleaned up her mess, so he doesn't know what she did.* That seemed like a plausible explanation. Meanwhile, she was embarrassed to tell her housemates about the run-in with Jolina, so she didn't say anything.

Marge made a special birthday dinner for her. Brianna breathed in the tantalizing scent of home-cooked food as candles flickered on a silver candelabra on the table. A symphony of praise music played in the background.

Afterward, Wayne led a prayer asking for God's blessing on her coming year. Next, Marge brought in a stack of gifts wrapped in pretty paper. Warm winter gloves. A scarf and matching knit cap. The largest box contained a down coat from Kate.

"How can I thank you?" she asked, as she remembered a scripture that described her situation. "For I was hungry and you gave me something to eat, I was thirsty and you gave me something to drink, I was a stranger and you invited me in.' You three have done that for me."

The next morning, she considered calling Tiny, but had no clue what to say. *"Hi Tiny. Are you aware that your mother threw cake in my face?"* No, she'd give him more time.

She decided to follow Amber's final advice. "When you pray about this, give it into God's hands and don't take it back. Test faith and see how it works."

*Lashing out would be much easier*, Brianna thought, anger rising in her. Instead, she turned up the praise music that Amber had loaned her. Then, she went to work on Martha's Room.

She tore out the gold wall-to-wall carpet by herself. Then, Kelly and Amber came over to help her drag it downstairs and haul it to the landfill.

Amber had told Kelly about the cake incident, so when Brianna had a few moments alone with him, she quietly asked, "What is wrong with Tiny's mother. And why doesn't he call me?"

Kelly listened sympathetically. "He's in a hard spot. As you now know, his mother has mental health issues. I think Tiny is so tired of dealing with her that he tends to ignore her problems. And Brianna, if he knows about the cake, he's probably too embarrassed to call you."

"You're right. That would be so humiliating." Her heart melted toward Tiny.

Time flew by as she waded into the labor-intensive renovation. She was on a first-name basis with the owner of Hammer's Hardware Store in Cottonwood City. She had even put the store on speed dial. Everything she could buy locally saved her a trip to Bismarck. Besides, she liked helping the local economy.

"I was destined to be in hardware," Mel Hammer had told her when she commented on his name. "Having a name like Hammer, what else could I do but sell tools?" Mel had ordered in a special hardwood floor refinishing kit for her.

The floor in Martha's Room had a few scratches and nail holes, but mostly it needed cleaning. The kit promised the project could be done in a day. It had taken twice as long, but the results were worth it. The rich dark wood warmed up the room.

Next, she and Amber had painted the ceiling a creamy white, and the walls and closet bayberry. She thought the pale green was quite pleasing against the dark woodwork of the large window and doors.

Meanwhile, she'd dragged the original Turkish area rug down from the attic. When she laid out the muted beige and green rug on the front lawn, she knew it was a real find.

Traffic seemed particularly heavy that afternoon, perhaps because it was a beautiful Indian summer day. Fall leaves were in their prime, the sky was cloudless, and insects buzzed in the warm air. On the other hand, perhaps it was because people heard that the woman from San Fran had dragged an old rug to the front lawn of Kate Schulte's house.

Several stopped to offer Brianna advice. "Tell Kate to spring for a new rug," one woman said. Another suggested turning the garden hose on it. The fellow from Cottonwood Antiques wanted to take it off her hands.

Brianna decided she had nothing to lose in trying to restore the carpet. She let it air for an hour before borrowing Wayne's shop vac. After another hour, it looked better. Then she tested it to see if the colors would run. When they appeared to stay fast, she got down on her hands and knees and began to spot clean it.

She sighed. The carpet looked clean now, but it still smelled like the attic. Marge had the solution. She covered the rug with a box of baking soda from the kitchen and vacuumed again.

Just as she finished, a shriek came from the veranda.

"Brianna Davis! What are you doing to my rug?" Kate was leaning on her cane, a shawl about her shoulders. She shook with anger. "I wondered why there was so much traffic out here. Have you lost your senses? You've drawn a crowd and ruined my rug!"

Brianna coolly turned to face Kate.

"Excuse me? This rug has been in the attic for what? Thirty years? Either we're giving it a second chance or it's going for a ride to Cottonwood Antiques." Brianna's voice was brittle, one brow arched. "Look at it, Kate! It's beautiful and we're putting it back in Martha's Room."

Kate muttered something about impetuous women and stepped closer to examine the rug. "Well. Please be more discreet. 'Tis not right to air our lives on the front lawn for the entire county to see." With that, she let out a "Humph!" and stomped back into the house.

From the window, Marge smiled and shrugged her shoulders. Brianna took a deep breath. Although Kate had agreed to the concept of the B&B, she'd argued with Brianna over most of the changes. *At least it keeps me from thinking about Tiny and his mother. And my parents.* Her mother wasn't answering her phone calls.

It was late in the day by then, and Wayne walked across the street and offered to help her haul the rug back upstairs.

"Say, you wouldn't want to make a few more of those wooden wall hangings?" he asked once they were finished. "A couple people saw the first one while it was drying and word got around. Now several others have asked about them. I have plenty of wood scraps you could use."

Brianna was sore and bruised from the hard work of the past few days. Jontel hadn't sent any assignments from San Francisco lately, either. *Maybe I can take a day off and work on my art. I'd enjoy that more.*

"I can come over tomorrow and make some. There are more quotes I'd like to use." In just a few minutes, they made a verbal business agreement.

Wayne had been among the first in the region to set up a business website, and he made most of his sales of church furniture online. Now he agreed to supply the wood for the signs and sell the finished product. Brianna would do the creative work.

"I think you need a business name," he advised. "Your ideas for home decorating are going to take off."

"Davis Designs," she said impulsively. "That's broad enough to cover decorating and making signs. I need to ask you something else. I'm thinking about finding some different wheels. I could hardly get the paint in my Miata, plus I need something that's good for winter driving."

"I'll be on the lookout for something bigger. You want a minivan?"

*I'm not old enough to drive a minivan. I'd rather haul furniture on top of my car.* "No."

"I have an idea," Wayne's face brightened and then fell. "No, that wouldn't work. You'd never be interested in something like that."

"Like what?"

"It's funny. We ran into Hans Hanson's daughter last time we were in Bismarck. Hans died a couple of years ago, but he delivered milk here for decades. She was telling how she'd like to sell his panel truck. He kept it in tiptop shape. But you wouldn't want something that old."

"How old?"

Wayne chuckled. "As old as you. Says Cottonwood Dairy on the side. Not much of a market for milk trucks these days."

"I want to see it."

Wayne shook his head. "Oh, I don't think you'd be happy with it."

However, Brianna wasn't listening. In her mind's eye, she could see herself driving around the countryside in an old panel truck with the name of her business on the side. It would be practical, eye-catching, and definitely not boring.

"Could we look at it tomorrow?"

"That might be possible. I'll ask Marge to give the daughter a call. The truck is parked in a Quonset on the edge of Cottonwood City."

After Brianna cleaned up her mess in the yard, she went back upstairs to admire the carpet. She slid to the floor to survey the project, mopped her face with the sleeve of her denim work shirt and blew a strand of hair out of her eyes.

The cleaning had worked magic on the colors. *Another item rescued*, she thought. *Just like me. I was as lost as an old rug in an attic, but love saved me.*

Brianna's thoughts turned back to Tiny. She remembered the sweet words he'd written in her birthday card and his nickname for her. She fingered the necklace that hung around her neck.

For the past few days, she'd tried to seek the Lord as she went about her labor. In those times, she felt enveloped by God's presence. Whether she and Tiny had a future together or not, everything would turn out fine.

Now, she made a decision. She needed to find Tiny. Right now.

Chapter 14

# *The Cowardly Lion*

The church at Cottonwood Creek gleamed white in the morning sun, its spire pointing toward heaven. A field of sunflowers sat to the east. The golden grass of the south yard stretched to the cemetery. There, past parishioners lay beneath headstones of granite, marble, and hand-wrought iron crosses.

The creek crossed native prairie to the west of the church. The June grass and coneflowers were brown and withered as they waited for a blanket of snow.

A footbridge led across the creek from the church to the two-story cottage that had served as a parsonage for decades. It sat settled and welcoming among the leafless lilac bushes.

Tiny turned into the driveway on his way to meet with Kelly Jorgenson. He remembered the day Kelly had arrived to be pastor of the church. A crowd had turned out to help him unload the trailer he pulled behind his pickup. They also set up a big pot-blessing meal in the churchyard.

After drooling over the tables laden with homemade food, Tiny had slipped into the front of the line next to Kelly. He soon realized the new pastor didn't know the difference between fleischkuechla and kase kniphla. That probably meant he didn't know that a church meal was a serious competition. Everyone wanted to be known as the best cook or baker. *Did they teach preachers that in Bible school?* Tiny wondered.

As they went through the line, Tiny explained the rules of engagement. By the end of the day, a friendship had formed. The new guy might be a pastor, but he still needed a buddy. Tiny had taken Kelly fishing, hunting and bowling. He bought pizza and pop for the new youth group.

Now, Tiny needed Kelly's help.

"Hey Tiny, good to see you," Kelly greeted him in stocking feet. He wore glasses with thick lenses. "I'm studying, but could use a break. Come on in."

Tiny dragged himself up the steps. He noticed the parsonage kitchen was neat and homey. The bachelor pad vibes had disappeared since Kelly and Amber got married.

Kelly motioned him toward the breakfast nook. Tiny slipped into the seat. He could see Kelly's books spread all over the dining room table and that cat, Mildred, sprawled on top of them. Although he took care of Mildred while the couple had been on their honeymoon, Mildred didn't bother to greet him. He sighed, wishing he had the easy life of a cat.

"What brings you out here?" Kelly asked.

Where to start. So much had gone wrong so quickly. He figured Brianna had told Amber about the incident with his mother, and Amber had told Kelly. At least that part was covered.

He cleared his throat. "Thought you should know that Sheriff Pickle took Ma to the State Hospital in Jamestown this morning. She needs to be observed and to have her meds updated." Tiny's shoulders slumped as he thought about the ongoing battle to help his mother.

"I know she's been struggling," Kelly offered.

"Yep." They remained silent for a few moments.

"What do they say is wrong with her?"

"A long-winded term. Schizoaffective disorder. It covers a lot of things. For Ma it means she can't take care of herself and she obsesses over things. Medication helps for a while and then, as Bill says, she needs a tune-up."

He hung his head. No matter how hard he tried, it always ended up this way. Her illness ruled his life. "Sorry to drop this on you, but I gotta talk to somebody. I don't know how much more I can take. It looks like Ma ruined my chances with Brianna."

There, he'd said the thing that bothered him the most. All these years he'd taken care of his mother, plodding on without complaint. Now, he had finally been so close to a dream life of his own. Losing Brianna was like a nightmare, like falling backward off a ladder.

"I need to ask if your mother has ever been a danger to herself or others?"

Tiny recognized the professional question, reminding him that Kelly was in the business of helping people with problems.

"Yep." Tiny paused again. "A few times she's taken too many pills. 'Course, I'm never scared of her, but she gets strange ideas."

"About Brianna and the cake." A flicker of a smile crossed Kelly's face.

"Hey, the cake thing might sound funny, but it isn't to me. Ma hates Brianna. That's never gonna change," he grumped.

"Try to keep this in perspective. Brianna's this high-powered career woman, and the picture of her getting hit with a cake is funny."

Tiny still wasn't seeing the humor. "She was getting used to Cottonwood Creek, trying to fit in. Ma ruined it." *The game is over and I lost*, he thought.

Kelly looked sympathetic. "What did Brianna say when you talked to her?"

Tiny shrugged. "I haven't talked to her."

Kelly ran his fingers through his hair. "Then, don't call the game at half-time."

Tiny stared at him. It was as if Kelly was reading his thoughts about the game.

"Listen, I can't face her. How can I explain my mother?" Tiny's head sank to his chest. "Just call me a cowardly lion."

Kelly spoke quietly, but confidently. "Don't forget, the biggest problem the Cowardly Lion had was that he didn't believe in himself. He needed courage. Tiny, you need to believe in yourself. God does. He made you and He has a plan for your life."

Kelly jumped up and grabbed a Bible. "Over and over this book tells us to have courage. Have faith. Fear not. Man, you need to quit looking at the circumstances and start believing what God says. He's for you, not against you. He wants to give you, Tiny Winger, hope and a future."

"But how do I know that Brianna is part of God's will for me?"

Kelly bent over the book before him and thumbed through the pages. "Right here. Proverbs 3:5. 'Trust in the Lord with all of your heart and lean not on your own understanding. In all of your ways acknowledge him and he will direct your paths.'" He looked up, his glasses sliding down his nose. "Just trust Him."

Tiny looked up at the bill of his cap. "I guess even the Cowardly Lion had to face his fears. I could call Brianna. Hearing her say, 'Get lost' couldn't make it hurt any worse."

"That's the way. Have courage. Be bold!"

Tiny groaned.

"Listen, God is able. I didn't think I'd ever get over my brother's death. Sure, I still miss him, but it's as if the scar tissue is healed. A few months ago, Amber almost died, but today she's working on her new office, ready for the next stage of her life. Have faith."

"I don't know if Brianna will even see me." Tiny shook his head. "But, I'll try."

"Good. Let me know how it goes. Then about your mother. We need to pray for a breakthrough for her. Let's pray that God will heal her and restore her mind."

"Oh, that's not possible." Then Tiny looked intently at his friend. "Is it?"

Kelly smiled. "Possible, even probable. We have two prayer needs on the table. What do you say we pray right now?"

Later, as they walked to the door, Tiny remembered something he wanted to tell Kelly. "I just signed the lease on that empty space in the Taylor Building. I'm going to put some exercise equipment in there."

"Are you opening a gym?"

"I need a place to work out this winter and I thought others might like it, too. I still need to go to the bank and get some things in order, but, yep, I guess I am opening a gym."

"So what's this place going to be called?"

"Hadn't thought much about it. Maybe keep it simple. Tiny's Gym?"

"I like that. Tiny's Gym. Congratulations. Can I be the first to take out a membership?"

"Hey, I'll give you a lifetime membership."

Before he left to go back to the shop, Tiny paused, cap in hand. "Do you ever think about the way time marches on?" he asked. "It's strange how Ma's only been away for a few days and already I've begun a business. Wouldn't Ma be surprised?"

Then the smile faded from his eyes. The truth was she wouldn't care. He was on his own, and there was no use in trying to make it otherwise. It was just him and the Good Lord. And maybe someday, Brianna, too.

When Tiny left, he felt better. He decided to drive to Schulteville to see Brianna after he closed the co-op for the day. He didn't know what he'd say. Still, his heart told him this was the right thing to do.

Except, once again, Jolina interrupted his plans.

# Chapter 15

# *Many Thanks, Jolina*

Jolina Winger might have left the State Hospital after a couple of weeks if not for the misunderstanding. It seemed the staff wasn't too keen on her hobby.

Now, she wouldn't be going home any time soon and bitter thoughts filled her mind. She wouldn't forget the day Sheriff Pickle pushed her head down and made her climb into his car. The indignity of being hauled off by the sheriff still smarted. At least the backseat had a cage across it, so he couldn't touch her. She usually avoided men, except Tiny, of course.

Still, this "guesthouse" wasn't too bad. She'd stayed here before and the staff treated her fine. They spent time each day visiting with her, sometimes with machines attached to her head.

The staff served her meals right on time and were good about catering to her needs. If she had any money, she'd leave a tip for them, like they did at the hotels in her soaps. However, there hadn't been a moment's notice before Pickle hauled her off, so she had no money.

Sometimes she wished the staff wasn't quite so gracious. There was never a moment for herself, except during the night. The other guests were, well, let's just say she didn't have much in common with them. Forced to meet with a small group of people every afternoon, Jolina chose to sit silently and stare past everyone. For all they knew, she found the potted plant fascinating. They were a strange bunch, that was for sure.

In the past, Jolina had been hospitalized for a few weeks. During that time, she received a mental health evaluation and had her individual treatment plan updated. Staff monitored changes in medication for a few days before sending her home. She knew the routine and told them what they wanted to hear.

If only she hadn't missed her friends back home so much. If only she could have stuffed little Sassy in her bag, she wouldn't have been so lonely. Now, this "hotel" was home for the foreseeable future, all because of a misunderstanding.


Tiny was still at the Co-op when an email from Jolina's doctor arrived with a ping. He read it with mixed feelings. His frustration with his mother was over the top. As soon as the store emptied of people, he phoned the doctor. After hanging up, he shouted to Rusty to watch the shop for a while. Grabbing a pint of milk, he rushed out the door.

A gusty wind pushed against his pickup as he drove back out to the parsonage to see Kelly. He hunkered over the steering wheel and took a swig. After switching from soda to milk a few weeks ago, he was surprised at how much better he felt.

The news about his mother didn't surprise him. Sure, he wanted her to get well, but what were the odds? She'd been this way for years. Still, the news was unsettling. He never knew what would happen next where his mother was involved.

At Kelly's, he slumped at the table where he'd sat just a few hours earlier and slammed his hand down on the table. "Why can't I have a normal mother? I just found out Ma will be at the hospital for a long time."

Kelly jumped at Tiny's pent-up response. "It's okay. Calm down and tell me what happened." Kelly leaned on the table and looked intently at his friend.

Taking a breath, Tiny explained. "Her doctor contacted me. During the night, Ma stole a pair of scissors and began cutting up her drapes."

"Why would she do that?"

"Your guess is as good as mine. They already knew someone had been in the laundry room one night and destroyed some of the other patients' clothes."

Kelly groaned.

"They found scissors hidden in her room. She likes a good pair of scissors."

"That's disturbing."

"What's worse is when they tried to throw the ruined curtains away, she had a fit. Kept saying something about being sassy."

"This is a tough turn of events," Kelly agreed. "You're going to need more of that courage we prayed for."

"So, what's the opposite of having courage?" Tiny asked.

"Being discouraged."

"That's me."

Kelly was lost in thought for a few moments. "Look, I can understand why you'd be discouraged. You've been through this before. But, what is the worst thing about this for you?"

"This time, just one word: Brianna. We were building something together, but Ma wrecked it. What's Brianna going to think when she finds out Ma's so bad off they plan to keep her in the hospital for a long, long time?"

"Maybe it's a good thing that she'll be gone longer. It gives you more time to figure out your relationship with Brianna. Maybe you should say, 'Many thanks, Jolina.'"

Tiny brightened. "That's true. We'd probably have all winter to spend time together, if she'll even speak to me."

Kelly smiled. "Make the most of it, buddy!"

"Hey, I'll give it a try. I sure wish I could see into the future."

"Maybe we can't see the future but God can. I believe he'll make a way for you."

# Chapter 16

# *It's My Fault*

A steady stream of customers kept Tiny busy at the Co-op for the rest of the day. After closing at six, he went home and paced the floor for a few minutes. The house was quiet and empty without his mother sitting in front of the blaring television.

Tiny took a fortifying breath and picked up the phone. Then waffled. *I should call Brianna. First, I'll sort the mail. Maybe it would be better to drive out there, but I need to take a shower first.*

"What am I supposed to do?" he yelled at God. "Just forget the whole thing? Pretend we never met?" *Pretend we never kissed?*

The thought of kissing her made his insides feel like marmalade. He couldn't keep arguing with himself. He put on his cap and jacket, and strode out the door. He was driving straight to Schulteville, no shower, no supper, no stops along the way.

***

Brianna surveyed the almost completed guest room. It wouldn't take long to hang the drapes, put artwork on the walls and make the bed. Their guests were due late the next afternoon and she couldn't wait to hear their evaluation.

Meanwhile, she had an overwhelming urge to see Tiny. A look in the mirror stopped her. She hardly recognized the person who looked back at her. A shower, makeup and a silk shirt would help her feel more relaxed and confident.

Half an hour later as Brianna came down the stairs, Marge stood expectantly by the dining room door. "Dinner's ready. You aren't going out are you?"

"Yes. I'm sorry I didn't let you know. Something came up." She whisked out the door before Marge could ask any more questions. Climbing in the Miata, she was soon on the narrow road to Cottonwood City.

At last, she was seeing things clearly. She didn't want to go on without Tiny. Her mother wouldn't approve. At all. Brianna didn't care. Working on a relationship with Tiny might defy her mother's logic, but everything in her said it was the right thing to do.

*Wasn't it the Olympic champ, Eric Liddell, who said he sensed God's pleasure when he ran?* Brianna mused. Well, she sensed God's pleasure when she was with Tiny. She pushed down on the accelerator as she considered what to say to him.

Brianna was so engrossed in her thoughts that she didn't notice the red light blinking behind her until Sheriff Pickle turned on the siren. Her mouth dropped open and she quickly pulled to the side of the road.

She was sitting there with her window down waiting for the sheriff to come to her door, when Tiny's pickup came over the hill.

"This is bad," she mumbled to herself.

Tiny pulled over and rolled down his window. "Brianna."

"Tiny."

Bill Pickle got out of the patrol car and walked up to her door, but turned and spoke to Tiny. "Winger, do you know this woman?"

"I do," Tiny said solemnly.

The officer looked like he wanted to frown, but couldn't

quite manage it. Turning to Brianna, he said, "Young woman, you were doing seventy in a fifty-five mile an hour zone. I need to see your driver's license."

"I'm so sorry," Brianna said, tears coming to her big brown eyes. She was looking at Tiny rather than the sheriff. "I should have told you right away what happened."

"It's my fault," Tiny said, peering around the sheriff. "I should have warned you about my mother. I let you walk into a bad situation."

"Listen, folks, you need to work out your private matters somewhere besides here on a public road. Can I see that license now?"

Tiny pushed his cap back on his head. "Meet me at my house?"

"I will," Brianna said passionately. "As soon as I'm finished here."

She looked at Bill Pickle and smiled sweetly. "Let me get my purse out and find my—."

"Never mind. I'll let you off with a warning this time, but keep your speed down."

After she drove off, the sheriff walked across the narrow strip of pavement to Tiny's pickup. "She's a keeper. Drive carefully. And good luck."

It was dark when they arrived at the house. Brianna peeked at the porch in the faint glow of a streetlight. Someone had cleaned up the space and her instincts told her that Tiny had taken care of the mess. Once inside the house, Tiny flicked on a ceiling light and Brianna looked around. The living room had paneled walls and a beige carpet. *Total remodel needed*, she thought. The centerpiece of the room was a burgundy recliner aimed at a huge television. An ashtray overflowing with cigarette butts sat on a side table.

Tiny grabbed the ashtray and dumped it in a trashcan located near the kitchen door. "Seems like I'm always cleaning up my mother's messes," he said as he turned to Brianna.

She noticed his eyes were the same blue as a velvet dress she once owned.

"I didn't have the guts to call you after what happened. I've been acting like the Cowardly Lion."

*Huh?* She cocked her head, trying to follow what he was saying.

"You know, like in the *Wizard of Oz* when the lion was afraid of everything. Kelly told me it was because the lion didn't have self-confidence. He said I needed some, too."

Tiny looked away. "Besides, I figured you'd never want to see me again."

"It's my fault, too." Brianna said quietly. "I shouldn't have come here without talking to you. I really brought the cake as an excuse to meet your mother. If you can forgive me, I think we should try to work things out," she whispered.

"You do?" Tiny's voice boomed in the quiet room. "Hey, hey, I can't believe it. That's great news. Of course I forgive you."

Brianna stepped over to him. When his arms went around her, she noticed that her head fit perfectly against his shoulder. When she looked at his face, he had tears in his eyes.

"I'm so happy we're together again. All of a sudden I'm hungry." Tiny continued to hold her. "Man, I forgot to eat lunch. That's a first."

"I'm hungry, too. Can we make a salad or something?"

Tiny looked up at the ceiling as he thought. "No lettuce in the fridge, but there's a box of mac and cheese in the cupboard," he said hopefully. "Or my famous sandwiches."

"I can't understand how you lost all of that weight eating mac and cheese."

"It wasn't what I ate that made me gain weight. It was how much." In the end, they ordered takeout from the diner and Tiny went to pick up their meal.

While Brianna waited for him to return, she studied a row of photos, the only wall décor in the room. Tiny at a young age. His graduation photo. A snapshot of his family blown up and framed. The final photo was of a young woman with long hair worn in a flip with an engaging pair of dimples. *Can that be Jolina?* She wondered.

Taking advantage of her time alone, she explored the house. The front bedroom was strewn with men's clothes and decorated with posters of sports cars. *Tiny's room.* On the other side of the house, an open door revealed a smaller bedroom. A worn lavender chenille spread covered the single bed. A few pieces of women's clothing hung in the closet. *Jolina's room.*

Brianna opened the door across the hall and flipped the light switch. A table sat in the middle with a sewing machine on it. Dolls covered every dresser and shelf. Walking around, she picked up the dolls made from bits of cloth, yarn, and ribbon. They varied in size and details. All wore colorful outfits, and had yarn hair and embroidered faces.

"These are wonderful," she exclaimed aloud.

"I always thought they were nice." Tiny stood behind her holding a take-out bag.

Brianna spun around. "Oh, you caught me snooping."

"I don't mind," he said with a shrug. "But Ma doesn't let anyone in her hobby room."

"Oh, please don't tell her I was in here. She already hates me."

"Ma wasn't like that when I was growing up. What you saw was her sickness talking. I hope the hospital can help her find her way back to the way she was."

Brianna turned and picked up a sweet little doll with

red yarn hair and a green dress. "Your mother is very talented. Has she ever tried to market these?"

"Are you kidding? That would be like selling her friends."

Brianna sighed. "I guess we won't go there then."

For the next several hours, they munched and talked. Tiny recounted some of Jolina's history. Brianna listened sympathetically, but wondered if Jolina would ever accept her.

Tiny tried to soothe her concerns. "When Ma comes home, they'll have her meds regulated. She'll be fine."

Brianna wanted it to be fine. This macho guy stood for the simplicity, honesty, and faith for which she longed. She wouldn't let Jolina's mental illness sidetrack her own hopes and dreams. To her very core, she sensed that she and Tiny had a bright future.

It was close to midnight when Brianna stood up and stretched. Looking out the window, she was surprised to see big snowflakes drifting from the sky.

"That is so beautiful. I can't wait to spend winter here." She turned and started to put on her jacket.

"First snowfall," Tiny commented. "It might be slippery and you haven't tested your little Miata on ice. I'll follow you home and make sure you're safe."

*Someone to watch over me.* "Tiny, that isn't necessary, but it's so sweet of you." She wrapped her arms around him and he buried his face in her hair.

"May I call you my Mango Queen?"

She answered with a kiss.

Chapter 17

# *Song of a Lark*

It was a sure bet that Brianna would attend the fall concert at Cottonwood High School. Both Tiny and Amber
had purchased a fist full of tickets for the event and the
whole town planned to turn out. Along with the excite-
ment of watching their children, grandchildren, nieces,
nephews and neighbors perform, they'd raise funds for the
music department.

"That's part of the hometown spirit," Tiny explained
to Brianna. "If you're in business, you help out wherever
you can."

"I get it! This is supporting the arts Cottonwood-style.
Slightly different than the cocktail parties my mother likes
to host." Brianna wrinkled her nose at the memory of her
mother's constant parties and galas. She'd often been en-
listed to hand out brochures or pass around plates of appetizers to guests.

Her mother never failed to put her on display, embel-
lishing her artistic skills and finagling compliments. "Isn't
my daughter beautiful," she'd coo to a complete stranger.
Sometimes Brianna felt like a salesperson's display model.

"Would you go with me to the concert?" Tiny asked,
tickets in hand.

"Sure. When and where will it take place?"

"Saturday at the school gym."

"A concert in a gym?" She pictured sweaty boys bouncing basketballs across the court.

"Yep."

"I love it. Students doing music in the school gymnasium."

The grand opening of Amber's insurance office was set for the same day as the concert. Brianna and Amber spent the morning putting the final touches in place.

The coffee and hot apple cider had just finished perking when the door opened and Amber's first visitors arrived. Brianna busied herself unwrapping trays of cookies, while Amber greeted her guests. A steady flow of people stopped in to pick up a calendar and wish Amber well. Brianna could see Amber was proud of the calendar, which advertised Gates Insurance North and featured homey scenes, that so represented her way of life.

Brianna had put a lot of thought into the wall hangings for Amber's office and then worked late into the night to finish them. She focused on the concept of "peace" and "peace of mind" since certainly they were the essence of why people bought insurance.

There were business cards in her pocket. If someone liked the office decor, she could promote Davis Designs.

The open house ended late in the afternoon, giving Brianna just enough time to drive back to Schulteville and change clothes. She had dressed up for the open house, but now she chose casual black slacks and a pink turtleneck sweater. When Tiny arrived, Marge served them all Indian tacos, and then they scooted out the door.

Tiny kept glancing at Brianna as he drove. "You look beautiful tonight. That pink sweater—." He didn't finish his sentence.

"It's hot pink," she teased him and, sure enough, his ears turned as pink as her sweater.

"Wow! The whole town must be here," Brianna said when they got to the school. The parking lot was full, so they squeezed into a spot a block away. She was glad she'd ordered a pair of flat-soled boots to walk on the icy sidewalk. Linking her arm through Tiny's she felt at home, like a member of the community.

"There's so many people here, we may have to sit in the bleachers," Tiny commented.

"Really? They pull out the bleachers for a concert? Outstanding! We should try to sit as high up as we can."

Of course, even with all of the people packing the gymnasium, Brianna caused a stir in her hot pink sweater and long dark hair. Tiny seemed proud to be at her side. Scanning the crowd, she waved to a dozen people that she recognized. They waved and smiled back.

Then the students began to file on stage and take their places on the risers. The girls wore black dresses in various styles, while the boys had on black dress pants, white shirts, and ties. The band members, dressed similarly, came in and sat to the side of the stage in semicircles of chairs. Some of the students looked familiar because they attended Kelly's church.

It hadn't been that long since she was in high school, and yet these kids seemed so young. Brianna smiled as she watched some of the girls clomp across the stage in platform heels and too much makeup. Instead of dress shoes, a few boys wore high-topped tennis shoes and they were obviously just learning to tie neckties. Lean faces sported notable cases of acne.

She didn't know the woman who led the choir, but she recognized the band director as the fellow who played keyboard at Kelly and Amber's wedding. Now he raised his baton, the lights dimmed, and the audience hushed.

The band got off to a shaky start at the downbeat. Then the choir came in somewhat discordant. The audience held its collective breath. However, within a few bars, the sounds began to blend. Nodding along, Brianna picked out the soprano, alto, tenor and bass sections.

Brianna knew the song. She reached for Tiny's hand and gripped it tightly as emotions welled up in her chest and threatened to spill from her eyes. The Rogers and Hammerstein show tune, *You'll Never Walk Alone*, was sung at her high school graduation after Kyle was killed.

She was numb with shock and grief after his death, so the song had hardly registered then. Now something, perhaps adrenalin, poured through her. *When you walk through a storm hold your head up high.*

That long-ago evening, she had kept her back straight and her chin high throughout the endless ceremony. However, inside she was screaming in pain. *And don't be afraid of the dark.*

Brianna's lips moved with the song. Those days had been the blackest of times, with no hint of light. She had been certain the years of grief would never end. *At the end of a storm there's a golden sky and the sweet silver song of a lark.* The words had seemed like a pointless promise back then.

Brianna closed her eyes and slowly shook her head from side to side, as she gave herself to the moment. *Walk on through the wind, walk on through the rain, though your dreams be tossed and blown.*

She'd done that day after day, year after year, while always longing for Kyle. *Walk on, walk on with hope in your heart, and you'll never walk alone.*

Now, she could no longer hold in her emotions. A sob escaped her, followed by a hiccup. Tiny, in a first-ever show of public affection, put his arm around her.

It had taken her too long to find out she wasn't alone, that God had been with her through it all. He had never left her side. Now, the biggest storm of her life was in the past.

"Tiny, it's true," she whispered. "No matter what happens, we are never alone."

He patted her shoulder, reassuringly. Though he didn't know why she was crying, he looked as if he might shed a few tears, too.

Taking a deep breath, Brianna searched her purse for a tissue. She needed to break one of her mother's social rules and blow her nose in public. A woman seated nearby turned and offered her a wad of tissues and a sympathetic smile. Instead of coolly staring past the woman as she might have in the past, Brianna looked her full in the face, sharing her naked emotions.

When the last chord of music ended, Brianna jumped up from the bleachers and began to clap loudly. Following her lead, Tiny stood up, and then the people around them rose to their feet. Soon the whole audience was applauding, the sound thundering under the metal ceiling.

On stage, young faces shone with surprise and joy at the response to their first number. They stood a little taller and sat a little straighter. It was a moment that many would remember for years. For Brianna, it was a turning point. She wouldn't ever feel totally alone again.

Chapter 18

# *Benediction and Blessing*

Outside the school, Brianna and Tiny met up with Amber and Kelly. The next thing she knew, Brianna was riding in the Jeep with Amber, while Tiny and Kelly went to pick up pizza.

"So what's going on?" Amber asked as she drove slowly along the highway that led to the parsonage. "You have raccoon eyes. Either the concert was quite moving or Tiny hit you."

"What? Oh no!" Brianna flipped down the visor and stared into the lighted mirror. Turning her head, she saw black circles under her eyes and tear tracks running down her cheeks.

"I need to find a cosmetics store that sells waterproof mascara." She took one of her remaining tissues and began dabbing her face. After trying to clean off the worst of the mess, she sighed and began to tell her friend what had happened.

"The first few years after Kyle died, I just went through the motions of living. I ate, slept, and went to school, but my heart felt dead. We had all these plans and dreams. All of a sudden, I was eighteen and alone.

"Things improved after college. It helped to move to San Francisco and begin a career. But, I found out you can have everything and still feel empty."

Amber spoke up. "That's when you decided to follow Kelly out here." Amber and Kelly had just found each other when he'd received a frantic call from Brianna. Because she didn't know Kelly well, Amber had to decide whether to trust his claim that Brianna was only a friend.

"Yes. He was a rocking role model and I wanted whatever he had. I'm sorry if I caused a few tense moments between you and Kelly."

"It was a little stressful, yet something good came out of it. I chose to trust that Kelly was telling the truth and that helped build our relationship. But what happened tonight?"

"There will always be room in my heart for Kyle, but I've moved on. Then tonight that song, *When You Walk through a Storm,* brought all of my emotions out again."

Brianna's mouth turned down and tears rolled from her eyes again. "Our class chose that song as a tribute to Kyle at our graduation ceremony. I hadn't thought about it in years, and then when those kids sang it tonight, I lost it."

"Oh dear," Amber responded. "I thought Kelly looked a little glassy-eyed, too. I'll have to ask him about it."

"In a way, I'm glad it happened even though I was humiliated in public. The words are so powerful. We will walk through storms, but we'll never walk alone. There is an end to the storms of life. It was so sweet and powerful, like a benediction."

Brianna's emotions felt rung out, but at least her tears began to dry up.

"Perhaps it was a benediction on the past and a blessing on your future."

"A benediction and a blessing. I like that idea!" Brianna said. "Amber, did you know Tiny and I have decided to begin dating? We'll need to deal with our parents, but we want to be together. We're going to trust God will help us with the challenges."

Amber tooted the horn and speeded up. "Praise the Lord! That's wonderful. Kelly and I hope you'll get married and live here. We can do life together!"

At the parsonage, Amber turned on the oven. The guys were on their way with a frozen pizza.

"I think this calls for a happy dance. Life is short, handle with joy," Amber said as she turned on her CD player. Upbeat Christian music began to play.

"That sounds like a phrase for one of my signs," Brianna said as the two women began making moves they'd learned in aerobic exercise classes.

"You're welcome to use it. How's your sign business going?"

"I'm surprised how many orders Wayne brings in. It's keeping me occupied, and I'm loving every moment I can work on my art."

Both women collapsed on the couch when the song ended.

"Now that the open house is over, I need to concentrate on getting ready for Thanksgiving. You and Tiny are invited. And Aunt Kate, and Marge and Wayne."

"That sounds like fun. I'll talk to Tiny and the others. Is your family coming, too?"

"Yes. My whole family will be here. And guess what, Adam is bringing Lori. There's another romance that's heating up. Cole will be staying here over Thanksgiving break, and I hope his grandma, Sadie, can come out of the nursing home for the day."

"You're going to need a giant-sized turkey!"

"Brianna, do you realize how many wonderful things happened this year? Kelly and I were married. My mother's multiple sclerosis is in remission. I survived the accident and am well. You moved here, and you and Tiny are an item. We have new businesses. The list just goes on and on."

"God is good."

"All the time."

Just then, the door flew open and two familiar pizza delivery guys walked in.

Long into the night, the foursome sat around the dining room table discussing their full and significant day. Stories were traded about Amber's open house. Talk of the concert brought tears to all of their eyes. Then they moved on to the work they were doing. Kelly's ministry continued to expand as Cottonwood Church reached into the community. Amber, Brianna and Tiny talked of the tests and trials of launching new businesses.

The last crust of pizza had grown cold, the music had long since quit playing, and now even the hum of the furnace silenced. They sat quietly for a moment, aware of being together at the beginning of a grand life adventure.

In the hush of the moment, Kelly stood and laid a hand on Amber's shoulder. Those at the table spontaneously linked hands and bowed their heads.

"Lord, we commit Gates Insurance North to your care and ask that through Amber and through the agency, many people will be helped."

Next, he moved to Brianna. "Your ways are marvelous, Lord. We couldn't have guessed your plans for Brianna. Now we pray that you'll expand her business to be a blessing to her and this community."

Finally, he laid his hand on Tiny's head, but instead of praying, he began laughing. Everyone looked up at him, curious smiles forming on their lips.

"Tiny, there's a scripture from Ephesians 3 that came to me. I think God has plans for you that you can't even imagine."

The others murmured their approval of Kelly's thoughts before he continued. "Now to him who is able to do immeasurably more than all we ask or imagine, according to his power that is at work within us, to him be glory.' That's my prayer for you, Tiny."

Brianna looked at Tiny, whose face was lit up with emotion.

"Nobody ever said nothing like that to me before," Tiny finally stated. "Thank you."

"Well, thank God," Kelly said. "I believe he's working in all of our lives."

With that benediction, the party ended. Still, they would long remember the night and see it as a sacred moment when they committed their works to the Lord.

Almost two hundred miles away, Jolina pulled embroidery scissors from her pajama pocket and began the difficult task of cutting up her bedsheet.

# Chapter 19

# A Sweetheart of a Deal

Brianna would never forget the day Wayne took her to see the old milk delivery truck. Marge had shooed them out the door with a promise to open Wayne's carpentry shop, turn on the lights, and make some coffee. She'd wait on customers and chat with those who just stopped by to gab.

On the way to Cottonwood City in Wayne's pickup, Brianna decided she had to ask a question that seemed silly. Everyone else apparently knew the answer.

"What exactly is a milk truck?" she asked Wayne.

"Haven't you ever heard of a truck that delivers milk around town?"

"It's new to me. We moved around a lot. Never got too settled anywhere."

Wayne gave her a sad sideways glance. Still, he seemed happy to tell her all about it.

"Farmers used to take their milk into town to the creamery. There the milk and cream were bottled. They made butter, cottage cheese, and ice cream, too. Then, early in the morning a truck drove around delivering bottles of milk to homes in Cottonwood City and Schulteville. Hans Hanson was the delivery guy. 'Course the local creamery's been closed for years now."

"How did he know what to deliver?"

"Oh, everyone had a metal box. In the early years, they'd put out their empty glass bottles, along with an order slip. Hans picked up the empties and left the milk in the box. Later, they switched to cardboard milk cartons."

"So they recycled. Interesting. Everyone must have known and trusted Hans Hanson."

"You couldn't find a better person. He went into the military right after high school and served in France in World War II. After the war, he married his high school sweetheart. Ines Ingelsted. Started delivering milk."

Brianna sighed. "That's a sweetheart of a story."

"It gets better. Nobody but he and his wife knew how he helped liberate France. After they both died, their daughter found his medals and some articles written about his heroism. Hans wasn't the kind of person that liked publicity. I guess he just wanted to lead a peaceful life."

"Sounds like he was a hero during and after the war. I hope the truck works out for me. I'd feel privileged to own it."

"Brianna, I think Hans would be thrilled to know someone really wanted his truck."

When they arrived in Cottonwood City, they stopped at Hammer Hardware, where Mel kept a key for Hans Hanson's building. Anyone who needed to get into it could borrow the key from Mel.

*Outstanding.* She thought about the network of trust among people that had lived and worked near each other for generations. Even more amazing, when she asked Mel for the keys to the truck, he laughed. "They're in the truck."

When they arrived, Wayne unlocked the padlock and rolled the big doors open. The day was cloudy and the electricity for the building was turned off, but she could still see the lifetime of tools and machinery that Hans had collected.

She strolled around, asking Wayne about each piece. An old-fashioned hay rake with a metal seat, horse harnesses hanging from the wall, a coil of copper. It made her realize how little she understood about rural life.

The milk truck was in the center of the dirt-covered floor. She walked around it.

"This is the cutest thing I've ever seen!" It was boxy, and the front looked like a person with big eyes and a jaw that stuck out. The passenger side opened like a bus door. Wipers pointed downward over the square front windows. She couldn't wait to turn them on and see them swipe across the glass. A side panel with the words "Cottonwood Dairy" was the perfect place for putting her own name.

"I'll take it. Whatever it needs will be worth it."

Wayne chuckled. "Not so fast. We better see if we can even start it." He circled the truck and noted that all of the tires needed air. Sliding into the driver's seat, he turned the key, while Brianna watched from the side. The engine sighed once.

"Good thing I brought the jumper cables along," Wayne explained. "The battery is dead." He pulled his pickup into the Quonset facing the old truck and made some connections.

"While we wait for the battery to charge, I'll pump up the tires and put some fresh gas in the tank. Why don't you try to reach Hanson's daughter and talk about a price? Tell her to keep it reasonable, because at this point it doesn't even start."

"You're a real jack of all trades," she said. "Thanks for taking the time to help me again. I couldn't do this without you." *What would I do without Wayne's help?* she wondered. *That's easy, I'd be forced to buy a minivan.*

Another thought lurked in the back of her mind. She and her father got along okay, but she couldn't remember him taking the time to help her as Wayne was doing right now.

An hour later, she had made a tentative deal and Wayne had the truck started. She proudly climbed in the cab and shifted into Drive. Pressing her foot to the gas pedal, she inched out into the light and stopped. Then they walked around it again.

"Needs new tires and a good tune-up. Tiny and Rusty can do the job for you." Wayne paused. "If that's still what you want. Are you sure you wouldn't like a nice minivan?"

Brianna shook her head. She loved this old truck. She noted that it needed some bodywork and new paint. Tugging open the back door, she was happy to see shelves lining the sides and plenty of space in the middle. A good cleaning, some new seat covers, and she'd be in business.

Brianna climbed in and drove toward town while Wayne locked up the Quonset. *If my mother could see me now in this dusty old truck, she'd think I'd gone off the edge*, she thought. What her mother might never understand was how happy Brianna was with her new life.

Her cute truck was a beauty. She could picture it with a new paint job. "Davis Designs" written in script on each side. The *Cottonwood Times* would surely run a story about the vintage truck and her new business. As she drove into town, she decided if she were interviewed, she'd be happy to say how much she loved living at Cottonwood Creek.

Just then, she felt something run up her leg. She gasped as a mouse ran across the dashboard and jumped to the seat beside her.

"Ah! Ah! Ah!" she screamed as she jerked to a stop at Your Friendly Co-op. She pushed against the door, but it didn't open. She was trapped! There were probably hundreds of mice in the truck. Laying on the horn, she screamed until Tiny and Rusty came dashing out of the shop.

Tiny pulled open the door. "Woman, what is the problem?"

Still screaming and crying, she leapt into his arms. "Mice. Mice everywhere. One ran up my leg." She was thankful she had slim pants tucked into boots. Otherwise, it might have run up her bare leg. She shuddered.

"Oh, Bri, it's all right. They won't harm you."

"What do you mean, they won't harm me? Those filthy mice are all over my new truck."

"Your truck? You bought Hans Hanson's truck? Sweet."

She grabbed his shoulders. "Tell me I didn't make a mistake."

"You did the right thing. We'll take care of the mice for you," Tiny said. "And the sticky door handle."

Brianna backed away and swiped at her clothes, hoping there weren't any more rodents on her. She patted her hair, and then looked up to see Tiny and Rusty exchange amused looks.

"This is not funny!"

It seemed inevitable that a small crowd formed. A couple who had been filling gas stayed for the show. Several school kids, on their noon lunch break, watched the unfolding drama. A woman pulled in off the street.

Tiny, Rusty and the high school boys began looking for mice in the engine and cab. Then the woman who had driven up took Brianna's arm and moved her away from the truck.

They stared at each other for a moment. "You're the one who gave me tissues at the school concert," Brianna said.

"Yes." She held out her hand. "Mona Hamilton. I'm the reporter, ad manager, and co-owner of the *Cottonwood Times.* Sometimes when a vehicle is parked for a while, mice move in and build nests. They probably came out when the engine warmed up."

Her words didn't help. "*Nests* of mice?"

"Don't worry, the guys can clean them out. Why are you driving Hans' truck anyway?"

Brianna's voice quavered as she explained that she was starting a new business and needed a bigger vehicle.

"Are you Brianna Davis, the woman from San Francisco that drives the little red sports car? Nice to meet you. This will make a great story."

Brianna was mortified. She could imagine the headlines. "City woman terrified of mice" or perhaps, "New business sees rodent infestation." She desperately hoped Mona was a feature writer and not interested in sensationalism.

Tiny walked over and greeted Mona. "Hey, I see you met Brianna. Not often we have someone move here who starts two businesses. Kate's B&B and Davis Designs. You were out of town and missed the grand opening at Gates Insurance North, but she helped decorate the office. You ought to stop by and see what they did with it."

"I am glad to meet you, Brianna," Mona said. "Welcome to Cottonwood Creek."

"I'm going to ask her to help me set up a gym in the Taylor Building," Tiny added shyly.

This was news to Brianna.

"You're opening a gym?" Mona scribbled in her notepad. "You two are quite the entrepreneurs. I'll be in touch with both of you."

After she left, Brianna beamed at Tiny. "She didn't even take a picture of the mouse-infested truck. You're a good public relations man."

"At your service," he said, touching his green cap.

# Chapter 20

# *Crazy Ideas*

**B**efore Brianna left the Co-op, Tiny invited her for supper at his house the next evening. He'd encouraged her to wear walking shoes so they could go for an evening stroll.

When she arrived, the fragrance of roasting meat wafted from inside. "Hello?" Brianna called as she let herself in. "Tiny, whatever you're making smells terrific."

Her last nutritional food packets were wasting away in the back of the fridge in Schulteville. While she had gained a couple pounds, the physical labor she'd been doing at the bed and breakfast helped keep her fit and slim. Besides, without her mother pressuring her, it was easy to slip into a different lifestyle.

Tiny peeked around the kitchen door. He had a giant white dishtowel tied around his waist and a spatula in his hand. "The grub is almost ready. Hope you like it, 'cause it's one of the only meals I'm good at making."

Living in the city, she hadn't needed culinary skills. She either ate out or pulled prepared food from the fridge. However, it was different out here. People ate more meals at home because there were fewer restaurants and grocery stores. It was a lifestyle she wanted to adopt.

Tiny took off his makeshift apron and gave her a hug. "You look beautiful," he said as he gave her a peck on the cheek. "Ma'am, let me show you to your seat."

To Brianna's surprise, the little dining room table was set with a plastic tablecloth, a matched set of dishes, and a stub of a candle in the middle.

"You've outdone yourself," she said as she sat down.

Tiny disappeared into the kitchen and returned with a sizzling baking dish and a bowl of wild rice. Next, he appeared with a container of coleslaw and a jug of milk. After he sat down across from Brianna, they bowed their heads and he said a simple prayer.

"God is great and God is good, Let us thank Him for our food; By His blessings we are fed, Give us Lord, our daily bread. Amen."

"Amen," Brianna echoed as Tiny scooped meat from the baking dish onto her plate and then onto his own.

She picked up her fork and took a bite. "Good chicken. Delicious," she said. "Has a little different flavor."

"It's not chicken."

"What is it?"

"Wild duck."

Brianna choked and then grabbed her glass of milk.

"Please don't tell me you shot these poor beings."

Tiny shrugged modestly. "Yep. I go duck hunting every fall. Goose and pheasant hunting, too. If you bite into something hard, it's probably a BB."

"What is a BB?"

"See the shotgun shells have little pellets that I call BBs. They scatter when you shoot the gun. Sometimes one or two will hide in the meat."

Brianna laid down her fork. Just when she thought they would have smooth sailing, some issue like this would pop up. She strongly believed in protecting animals.

"Tiny, don't you know about animal rights? You can't just go around shooting them."

"Why not?" Now Tiny laid down his fork. "Are you telling me you've never eaten duck in your whole life?"

She had. Duck was a specialty of a restaurant she frequented in San Francisco.

"That's different."

He leaned back in his chair. "How is it different?"

Brianna struggled to find an answer. "I, I guess I've never considered how the duck arrived on my plate." The truth was she liked duck and had ordered it a number of times. Suddenly, she felt like a hypocrite. She needed either to become a vegetarian or accept where meat came from.

Tiny helped her along. "You know in the Bible, God provided quail to the Israelites. That tells me it's okay to eat meat."

"True."

"This is good protein," he said, stabbing some meat with his fork. "These ducks lived wild and free, like God intended. Someday I'll show you the beautiful sloughs and lakes where I hunt. The ducks and geese have a good life and then I come along and, bam, they find themselves in duck heaven."

Brianna couldn't help but smile. "Duck heaven, huh? Is that in the Bible?"

"Well, maybe not," Tiny conceded. "But, boy, there's a lot you don't know about wildlife management. The best sportsmen really care about the birds, and make sure they have plenty of feed and places to nest. Why don't you learn more before passing judgment?"

Brianna felt chastised. "I guess there is a lot I don't know. Will you teach me?"

"Sure. You can go hunting with me next year." Tiny smiled his most charming smile.

At the end of the meal, they went for a walk around Cottonwood City. When they got to the downtown area, he steered her toward the back of the Taylor Building. After unlocking the door to the space, he went in ahead of her and turned on the lights.

"What's this?"

"Welcome to Tiny's Gym. I guess I let the cat out of the bag yesterday. I didn't want to tell you until I got through all the paperwork, but that happened today."

"Outstanding. When did you get this idea? When will it open?"

"Hold on," Tiny beamed. I'll tell you all about it." They sat on the floor, backs against a wall, and Tiny dug out a bag of M&Ms for dessert.

He told her how he'd gotten the idea while on a walk after their first date. After looking into it, he found out the rent was reasonable. "The biggest drawback was the smell of hair spray and chemicals that come through the vent from Maggie's beauty shop. Hey, hey, but she'll have to put up with the smell of sweat.

"Sometimes in the last few weeks, I thought maybe I had socks for brains. There were so many state regs, licenses, and permits. I was about to give up when Sam Smith, the banker, gave me a pep talk. He told me, 'Be like a boxer and get back in the ring.' So I did. I had help from him and others. They said I actually worked through everything in record time."

"I can't believe you did all of this and I didn't know about it."

Tiny shrugged modestly. "This is a low-budget operation. I heard about a gym that is closing in Minot and I'm getting a deal on basic equipment. Maybe someday I'll add fitness training and those Zulu classes. First, I have to see if it will work out. If not, well, at least I can use the equipment to keep fit this winter."

"I'll join your gym."

"If you help me with decorating and advertising you can have the first year free."

Brianna began rambling on about what colors to use and where to put mirrors. Then realized Tiny was very quiet. Stopping mid-sentence, she waited for him to speak.

"There's something else I want to show you." He pulled her to her feet and, after locking up, led her around the block to a former car dealership.

"What do you see when you look at this building?"

"An old gas station?"

"When I was a kid, this place was deluxe," Tiny explained. "You'd drive under that canopy and old man Johnson would come out and fill your car, wash the windshield and check the oil. He didn't believe in self-service. See those curved windows? I used to look inside at the little model cars sitting on the window ledge."

Brianna shielded her eyes and peered in a window. Then they strolled around the building, noting its size and location right on Main Street.

"His son owns it now. He lives out-of-state and the word is he wants to tear it down."

"That would be a shame. This place has a lot of character."

"Here's what I wanted to talk to you about: I want to buy the building."

"This gas station? You're kidding."

"I won't do it unless you think it's a good idea."

"Why is my opinion important? I'm just starting out in business myself."

Tiny chose his next words carefully. "This feels like something bigger than just buying a building. I want you to help me. I want us to be 'The Tiny and the Mango Queen Dream Team.'"

"That is a crazy idea. Crazy with a capital C."

"Together we can do anything, Brianna."

Beyond Tiny's shoulder, she saw the moon, full and yellow, peeking over the top of the Taylor Building. Then, he wrapped his arms around her. Suddenly, the idea didn't seem crazy at all. His head was full of dreams, but his feet were solidly on the ground. He was a man who was going places. She wanted to go with him, even if they never left Cottonwood Creek.

Brianna smiled impishly. "I'm just crazy enough to say yes, I'll help you. If you have peace about making an offer on the building, then do it. Perhaps the owner would like someone to take it off his hands."

Tiny swayed her back and forth. "I'm so glad you understand."

He rested his chin on her head, seeming to search for his next words.

"Will you..."

*Is he going to propose?* Brianna's eyes went wide in wonder.

Chapter 21

# The Invitation

Brianna stared at the ceiling as she lay in bed thinking about the question Tiny had popped. She smiled now, but at that moment when he paused to consider what to say, she'd broken into a sweat wondering if he'd propose.

Instead, he'd invited her to the Fireman's Ball.

"The what?" she'd asked in confusion and relief.

"The Fireman's Ball. A fancy dance. We have a volunteer fire department, and this is their big fundraiser. I go every year and stand along the wall watching the couples dance. I've never asked anyone to go with me," he admitted.

Then he hung his head and muttered, "Why would you go with me, anyway? I don't even know how to dance."

"Yes, I'll go to the ball with you."

"People get all dressed up, but all I've got is my brown suit. That don't fit anymore." Tiny paused as her words caught up with him. "Wait. You will go to the ball with me?"

"I'd love to. Thank you for asking me. Now, tell me what you mean by all dressed up."

"Wow. This will be like the prom date I never had." Tiny's eyes sparkled.

"Do the men go white tie?"

Tiny looked up at his cap in thought. "The guys wear suits and ties, but I don't remember any of them with white ties. I suppose someone might have."

Brianna blew out a breath. "White tie is a very formal way of dressing with a black jacket with tails, a white shirt and white bowtie. It's as formal as a tuxedo."

"Nope. Not that fancy here. Probably couldn't wear

something like that with cowboy boots. Lots of guys wear expensive boots when they dress up," Tiny offered.

The insight helped. "Ah, I see. When is this event? Maybe we'd have time to go shopping for a new suit for you."

"First weekend in December. I'd be grateful if you'd help me find a suitable suit. Get it? Suitable suit. I'm a budding author."

Brianna winced.

Now as she lay staring at the ceiling in the dead of night, the whole scene was rather humorous. She felt certain that he had almost proposed and then lost his nerve.

*Just as well. I don't know how I would have answered,* she thought. They had a few things to settle before considering spending their lives together.

For one, she suspected there would be more surprises like the duck dinner. They were miles apart in their experiences and culture. *Opposites might attract, but how do people live with each other when they are so different?* she wondered.

Of course, their parents were a real issue, too. Something had to change if she were to be closely connected with Jolina. Someday the woman would get out of the mental ward and move back to Cottonwood City. Brianna wasn't sure she was competent to live alone. Did that mean they'd need to live with Jolina and take care of her?

The idea made her shudder. Neither could she imagine Tiny living at the bed and breakfast. Besides, he was on call at the co-op, so it was convenient for him to live in Cottonwood City.

Her parents were also a big question mark. Brianna couldn't imagine introducing her mother to Tiny. Her mother could finish him off with a searing look or lethal words. Her father had grown more emotionally detached through the years. Would he accept Tiny as a son-in-law? She had no idea.

Brianna turned in the four-poster bed. She could still see the moon, though it had moved far across the sky since her conversation with Tiny. It reminded her that she was far out on the prairie, in a place that was foreign to everything she'd known. At this point, she planned to make her home here and stay forever. However, what if the new wore off? What if she wanted to move back to a more cosmopolitan life? Would Tiny go with her?

After all her musings, she knew of only one way to find peace. "In every situation, by prayer and petition, with thanksgiving, present your requests to God." She'd learned that verse from Philippines 4 at her very first Bible study. Now she simply whispered her concerns to God.

Before long, she felt the tension in her body melt away, though she remained wide-awake. She lay fingering the hem of her silk pajamas and thinking about the evening. Tiny's venture into owning a business and buying the old gas station was quite surprising. No matter what happened in their relationship, she would always admire the strides he was making.

That reminded her of her own business projects. The first guests at the bed and breakfast had stayed free, but left a generous tip. Their comments were guiding Brianna and Kate as they redecorated the rooms for future guests.

The two sisters had exclaimed over the charm of the stately house. They made glowing comments about staying in Martha's Room, loving the window seat and fireplace. The remodeled ensuite bathroom received profuse praise. Marge's breakfast scones, scrambled eggs, locally made sausage, and Brianna's French press coffee, were a great finale to a wonderful stay.

However, they also had suggestions that made Kate sputter. Brianna had giggled until she snorted. After touring the rest of the house, they had both said "yuck" to the hall bathroom. They were also notably quiet when viewing the other guest rooms. They both eyed the yellow wallpaper throughout the house with some disdain.

One happy surprise took place when they asked to see the third-floor turret.

"Are you planning to rent this room out?" one asked as she surveyed the small space, now littered with books and papers related to Brianna's work in San Francisco.

"Possibly," Brianna hedged. With no bathroom on the third floor, she wasn't sure anyone would pay to stay there.

"I think you should make it available. Anyone who sees a photo of the house online will want to stay up in the turret. Decorate it as well as you did Martha's Room and people will pay a premium for it."

Brianna had a long way to go before the house was ready for business next spring. She planned to tackle one room at a time when winter came in earnest. She was glad she could put that project on hold, because she continued to receive lucrative assignments from San Francisco that kept her busy.

Also, orders for wall hangings came in daily. She now offered six different designs. With a supply of shipping boxes, she had arranged to ship orders out twice a week.

In addition, she had local clients. She hadn't charged for her work on Amber's office and she looked forward to remodeling Tiny's Gym, but any new jobs would be paying clients.

Although Brianna had a lot going on, it didn't feel busy to her. She still rose every morning for a walk or run in the wide-open countryside. The autumn scents and scenes refreshed her soul. Her prayer and Bible study times with Kate, Marge and Wayne nurtured her spirit.

Then her thoughts strayed to Tiny's question and a smile spread across her face as she snuggled deeper into the soft sheets. She was going to make sure Tiny never forgot this year's Fireman's Ball.

Chapter 22

# Girl in the Red Dress

Thanksgiving arrived so quickly that Brianna had to place a rush order on the cheesecake she promised to bring to Amber and Kelly's house. Two large creamy desserts arrived near evening on the Wednesday before the holiday.

"You ordered cheesecake?" Kate had sniffed. "I didn't know you ate anything that rich."

"My mother always ordered cheesecake for special holidays." Her voice trailed off at the memory. Even if her mother made her crazy, her formative years did have their sweet moments. "We didn't have anything as ordinary as pumpkin pie. Thanksgiving and Christmas were 'free' days. No counting calories."

She and Kate were at the dining room table eating a light dinner. With Marge and Wayne on their way to Florida, they'd decided to scrounge in the kitchen for what they wanted. Brianna tackled the last of her nutritional meals, while Kate had prepared a poached egg over toast, which she drenched in hot milk.

"Holidays now are certainly different than in my youth," Kate said. "My mother used fall produce to make pies for Thanksgiving. She used pumpkins from the garden and apples from our trees. We roasted the pumpkins and scooped out the inside before starting the pies. And, oh, we'd roast the pumpkin seeds for a treat."

"Sounds like a lot of work. What was the third kind of pie?" Brianna asked, trying hard not to look at Kate's poached egg floating in warm milk. The sight almost made her gag.

"Plum. We had so many plum trees in the area. She made plum pie, plum pudding, plum jelly and plum butter! We were plum tired of plums before they ran out." A look of longing came into Kate's eyes. "What I wouldn't give for one of Mama's plum pies again."

"Kelly wanted to take his parents and me to pick plums last fall," Brianna recalled. "Then, so much happened. Your brother died and the Twin Towers were attacked in New York."

"I miss Ted so much. It's hard to believe how life flows forward even when you think the world should stop when someone dies. But now, we must not dwell on the past and miss the wonders of today."

"Yes," Brianna agreed. "It's Kelly and Amber's first Thanksgiving together. They've put some thought and prayer into it. They want the day to be meaningful and fun. A new tradition."

"And what about you?" Kate asked, peering into Brianna's eyes. "Have you put some thought and prayer into your relationship with Tiny?"

Brianna didn't mind the questions. It was motherly of Kate to care. Her own mother, Helena, didn't even know about Tiny.

Suddenly, Brianna needed Kate's wisdom. "We're so different. Like chalk and cheese. Do you think we can have a future together?"

"Only you two can answer that, but with God all things are possible." Kate stopped for a moment and then leveled a challenge. "Please be careful not to break Tiny's heart. I'm quite fond of him. He was one of my special students." Her lips were pursed.

Brianna knew a warning when she heard one. Or was it a threat? Either way, she was unable to respond. She didn't want to hurt Tiny any more than she wanted to get hurt herself. Yet, they seemed unable to slow the pace of their relationship.

Brianna recalled that conversation a week later as she dressed for the Fireman's Ball. She slipped into her narrow, silky red dress and checked the slit in the side that went up to her thigh. Looking in the mirror, she arranged her long dark hair to flow around her shoulders, allowing diamond earrings to flash.

Although they'd had a few snow squalls, none of the white stuff had lasted through the sunny days that followed. No snow boots needed, she thought as she donned low silvery pumps. She reached for her faux white fur wrap, just as Tiny arrived to pick her up.

As he stood talking with Kate in the front hall, Brianna slowly came down the stairs, peeking to see him. When he and Kate looked up at her, the conversation was forgotten. Tiny's eyes traveled from her feet upward as she descended, until their eyes met in an electric gaze. She smiled widely. His eyes popped.

Her heart plunged to her toes as she appraised him. At well over six feet, Tiny was always an imposing presence, but tonight. Tonight, he looked magnificent in his dark suit, white shirt and red tie. Any extra bulk he still carried was hidden by the cut of the suit. Maggie had styled his flaxen hair long and wavy. He met her at the bottom of the stairs and enveloped her icy hands in his large warm paws.

"Hot Chihuahua!" he exclaimed. "I didn't believe you could look prettier than you did the first time I saw you, but—."

She squeezed his hands. "You look pretty beautiful yourself."

Brianna suddenly felt shy and Tiny's face turned red. Kate came to their rescue. She snuggled the white wrap around Brianna's shoulders and pointed them toward the door. "Don't stay out too late. I'll keep the porch light on for you."

The Fireman's Ball was being held at the community center, a building that housed an auditorium, city offices and, of course, the fire department. Brianna waited in the lobby while Tiny parked a block away. She watched as dozens of people two-stepped around the room to The Good Old Boys band.

As people saw her standing in her red dress and faux wrap, their eyes lit up in recognition. If only she knew who they were. *Nametags would help, but that would be silly when most of them are related, live near each other, or attended school together.*

When Tiny arrived, a murmur went through the crowd. Brianna spied a mirror across the way. Looking at the wavy image, she drew in a sharp breath as she stared at their reflections. With his new haircut and suit, Tiny looked like a different person. His posture and the easy set of his jaw gave him a confident look. She was certain others were also seeing him in a new light. Tonight was Tiny's debut.

Oblivious to the attention, he beamed at her and then steered her toward a corner where Craig and Mona Hamilton had set up a camera. As they waited to be photographed, Brianna felt content in her supporting role, a role that had distressed her with other men.

As she analyzed why she felt differently with Tiny, awareness emerged. Most other men wanted to benefit from being with her, but darling Tiny cherished her as a person.

Coming back from her reverie, she realized Mona was speaking. "If we were electing a king and queen of the ball, you two would win for sure." Instantly, Craig pushed the button on the camera, capturing their delighted and amused looks.

"Did you hear that?" Tiny asked, his voice filled with wonder. He smiled and greeted a number of people as he led her to the dance floor for a waltz. She was glad they had practiced dancing a couple times.

"Hope I don't step on your shoes," he said into her hair as they swayed to the music.

"Oh, Mr. Winger, you're exceptionally smooth on your feet."

"I remember this song," he continued. "Ma used to listen to it. *All I have to do is Dream.* The Everly Brothers."

The lead singer crooned, "When I want you in my arms, When I want you and all your charms, Whenever I want you, all I have to do is drea-ea-ea-ea-eam, dream, dream, dream."

"That could be our theme song," Brianna ventured.

"Our song. Yep, our song should be about dreams."

The band played a couple more slow songs, and Brianna found herself humming along to a sweet country tune. Her disdain for the earthy simplicity of the genre melted away. As they moved into a two-step, she abandoned her previous mindset and sang aloud with the band.

Just when the evening seemed perfect, a rock and roll number began. To Brianna's horror, Tiny began to flap around like Big Bird. Those dancing near them gave him plenty of room as he twisted and turned, flailing his arms wide.

After the song, she grabbed Tiny's hand and pulled him off the dance floor. Before long, the fire chief thanked everyone for their support and told a couple stories about calls they'd responded to during the past year. When an intermission was called, they looked at each other and shrugged.

"Let's get some fresh air," Tiny said as he quietly guided her to a side exit.

They strolled through the little park located next to the auditorium enjoying the refreshing, chilly air. The scent of autumn leaves permeated the park as they crunched toward a bench. In the background, she could hear the music as the auditorium door opened and people exited. However, they were alone in this quiet corner of the park.

As they sat on a park bench, Tiny pointed upward. "Look. You can see the Milky Way."

Brianna tilted her head back. The sky was a wonder of light fused with the black background. Had she ever noticed how many stars were in the sky? All of life seemed like a giant mystery as she considered their tiny planet compared to the size of the universe.

Finally, she looked down again and was shocked to see Tiny kneeling before her. He clutched her hands in his and looked into her eyes.

"Brianna Davis, I love you. I have ever since I first saw you. I always will. It would be my honor and privilege if you would marry me."

Surprise flooded Brianna as she looked into his hopeful, earnest eyes. She reached out and touched a stray lock of his hair. She still didn't have answers to the questions that kept her awake at night. Were they compatible enough to stay together forever? Could they overcome their parents' likely objections? Could she be content at Cottonwood Creek?

As if reading her thoughts, Tiny asked her another question. "I'm a simple man with a simple faith, but this I know: If God is for us, who can be against us?"

Brianna sighed. He was so much the kind of guy she wanted to marry. A real man's man, one who practiced his faith without pretense. Maybe she didn't need all of the answers to her questions, if she trusted Tiny and trusted God. She smiled.

"Yes."

"Yes? You mean yes, you'll marry me? For real?"

"For real," Brianna said as tears formed in her eyes. "For real and forever."

Then she leaned forward and kissed him with a tenderness that surprised even her. And there under the stars in the chill of the night they whispered about their love for each other and their dreams of the future.

# Chapter 23

# The Big Mistake

He had just made the biggest mistake of his life. That was for certain. Tiny's hands trembled as he pulled into Kelly and Amber's driveway. It was well after midnight and all of the lights were off in the parsonage. What was he doing here? He couldn't wake up Kelly to tell him what a fool he'd been.

Tiny let his head drop to the steering wheel in defeat, hitting the horn, which blared into the silent night. Immediately an upstairs light came on in the house. Tiny groaned as Kelly appeared in a window. Moments later, he hopped across the driveway in bare feet and a bathrobe.

"Tiny, what are you doing here? What's wrong?" Kelly asked as he climbed into the passenger seat.

Tiny laid his head back against the seat. "I just made the biggest mistake of my life."

"Oh man. What did you do? Rob a bank?"

"Of course not."

"Quit your job? Buy some swampland in Arizona?"

"No, no, nothing like that. Oh man, I asked Brianna if she wanted to get hitched." The words send a surge of power through his body, like the current from an executioner's chair.

Kelly chortled. "No kidding? You asked Brianna to marry you?"

"Yep."

"That's great news. I didn't know you were going to pop the question so soon."

"Me, either," Tiny said with some confusion. "Well, I had practiced what I might say someday. I just didn't know it would be tonight."

"You better tell me all about it." Kelly looked up at the house and waved to Amber, who had appeared in the window. She waved back and disappeared, likely going back to bed.

"I went to pick her up for the dance. And you know that mango-colored dress she wore for your wedding? You won't believe this. The one she wore tonight was even hotter. Red. Slinky." He raised his hands and made a wavy silhouette. "Made my knees turn to jelly."

"Brianna is beautiful."

"We get there, and I'm all dressed up in this monkey suit and she's in her red dress and everyone makes a fuss over us. Everyone. Then we began to dance real slow. Do you know women press themselves up against you when you dance like that?"

Kelly struggled to stop another fit of laughter.

Tiny continued, his voice brightening. "We danced every dance. I really got into those rock and roll moves. Then, we went over to that little park for some fresh air."

His voice became solemn with impending doom. "That's when it happened."

"What happened?"

"She was wearing this little white fur thing over her dress and her hair was so shiny. She was the most beautiful girl ever and she was with *me*, so I put my arm around her."

Kelly remained silent, engrossed in the story.

"I was trying to think what to do next, so I looked up. There was a jillion stars in the sky! We sat on a park bench watching the Milky Way and the next thing I know I'm on my knee asking her to marry me."

"Good job!"

"What do you mean, good job? It was the biggest mistake of my life."

"Oh," Kelly commiserated. "You mean she said no?"

"That's the problem. She said yes! Think about it. Hitched. Like a team of horses."

"Tiny, you're complaining to the wrong person. I got 'hitched' this summer and I've never been happier," Kelly said. "Don't you love Brianna? Don't you want to be with her?"

As Tiny fell toward the steering wheel again, Kelly reached out and grabbed him. "Easy buddy."

Tiny grabbed Kelly's arm. "I can't think about anything but her. Who am I to hook up with someone like her? My old man was the town drunk and my mother lives at the funny farm. I don't make much money and I probably never will."

"She's crazy about you. Hasn't she told you that?"

"Well, she has, but it's nice to hear it from you since you've been friends for so long."

"Brianna has a tender heart. She needs someone like you who can see that."

"You're right. She's real high-end on the outside, but inside Brianna is soft. I think she needs me. Maybe I didn't make a big mistake. Maybe I just took a big step."

"So, man up and marry the girl," Kelly said. "Your life will change a lot...for the better. You're a believer. This is a time to trust God to take care of the details."

For the first time, Tiny relaxed and smiled. "I can't believe I asked the Mango Queen to marry me. And she said yes."

***

When Brianna arrived home after the ball, she made a quick trip upstairs to get ready for bed and then rushed down to Kate's room. Peering through the glass doors to the library-turned-bedroom, she saw Kate asleep. Her snores sounded something like the engine of a bi-wing plane.

Brianna shook the older woman. "Wake up. I have news to tell you."

"What?" Kate woke and quickly sat up in bed. "What's wrong?"

"Nothing is wrong, but I have news. Tiny asked me to marry him."

Kate reached for her hand. "What did you say? Wait, crawl under the covers with me and tell me all about it."

Brianna gratefully slipped under the quilt. She was now clear about why the other women at the dance hadn't worn thin party dresses, and why she and Tiny had the little park to themselves. Her feet felt like two ice packs. "I said yes! Do you think I did the right thing?"

"I always remember that Saint Paul said it was better not to marry."

Brianna groaned. How could Kate come up with a lecture so quickly?

"I think Paul wrote that so we'd take the obligations of marriage seriously. He himself remained single like me." Kate had a hint of pride in her voice.

"That's a lot of food for thought," Brianna commented, regretting she'd woken Kate.

"But, don't fret. Marriage was God's idea. Now, tell me all about this evening," Kate said, seeming to realize she'd been sidetracked. She patted Brianna's hand reassuringly.

"It was a remarkable night. Tiny looked great all dressed up and you could see the esteem people have for him. Oh, Kate, we danced almost every dance together! Then at intermission we went out to get some fresh air." Brianna hardly took a breath between sentences.

Kate thought dances led to no good, especially when young couples slipped out at intermission. Furthermore, she would have been happier if Brianna had worn something sensible, like a sweater and long skirt. However, she managed to keep her opinion to herself.

"We went out to that little park by the auditorium and Tiny showed me the Milky Way. I did not know there are so many stars! I was looking up at them and all of a sudden, Tiny took my hands and asked me to marry him." Brianna finished breathlessly.

"I know you've been thinking about your relationship with Tiny. What made you decide to say yes tonight?"

"I have so many concerns. My parents don't even know I'm dating, and who knows what will happen with Jolina? However, the whole evening was so perfect. It felt like we belonged together and we had so much fun. Tiny really cemented it with something he said after he proposed."

Kate raised her eyebrows. She had seldom been privy to such personal moments.

"He said 'if God is for us, who can be against us?' Kate, I want to spend my life with that kind of guy. Someone who believes, who is kind and, well, if God is for us, he'll help us with the future."

Kate shifted her ample weight and Brianna lay her head on her shoulder. "Tell me I did the right thing."

"Oh, Honey, I think you and Tiny could make quite a team. Just make sure the good Lord is on that team, too."

# Chapter 24

# Princess Wedding Dreams

The evening after their engagement, Tiny offered to make supper. Brianna was hesitant to try his cooking again after the duck dinner, but she finally agreed to come if he promised to include fruits and veggies on the menu. She could always decline any suspicious-looking meat, and he assured her there would be plenty of vegetables.

She expected to begin planning their wedding, a moment she had always dreamed about. Brianna was a preschooler when Princess Diana and Prince Charles married. She still recalled Diana's measured steps as she walked up the aisle of St. Paul's Cathedral. Later she learned that ten thousand pearls were sewn into the ivory gown, and Diana pulled a twenty-five-foot train.

Brianna had asked for a bride doll for her birthday that year. It was the first hint of her interest in fashion. By the time she became a teenager, she'd sewn wardrobes for all of her dolls. Then she moved on to making some of her own clothing on her little portable sewing machine.

For years she'd planned to make her own wedding gown of silk, satin, lace and pearls. It would be perfect. After all, if you plan to marry only once, the dress must be exquisite.

In addition, she had clear ideas for the wedding cake, the color and style of the bridesmaids' dresses, and even for dinner table décor. And the music. Canon in D Major during the service. Strolling violinists for the reception. Smooth jazz during dinner. Then she and her true love would slip away in a limo to an elegant hotel for the night.

A honeymoon on some tropical island would follow.

Brianna smiled as she cruised into Cottonwood City. She didn't live in England, Cottonwood Church was hardly a cathedral, and Tiny wasn't a prince. *Did any of that matter*? She wondered. The 'wedding of the century' hadn't guaranteed a happy marriage.

A change as big as a Malibu mudslide had happened to her a year ago. Things that had seemed important, perfect and wonderful had fallen apart. Now, her new life felt solid and comforting. Her heart was healing, and filling with joy and peace. And Tiny was her prince.

Now she often searched the Bible, for it held the pattern for living. There were warnings in it, too. One seemed especially relevant for her. Matthew 7:26 stated, "Everyone who hears these words of mine and does not put them into practice is like a foolish man who built his house on the sand. When the rain came down, the streams rose, and the winds blew and beat against that house, and it fell with a great crash."

She shuddered. She might have married any number of men, but none of them fit the pattern as well as Tiny. He was rock solid.

Although he had his shortcomings.

"Pew! Stinky!" she said as she walked in the door of Tiny's house. A strong odor had drifted out the door when she arrived. Now it permeated the house. "What are you cooking?"

"Healthy food like you wanted. There's no better meal than sauerkraut, kniphla and sausage. It's my go-to meal when I'm hungry."

Brianna was speechless. She threw her coat on a chair and made for the stove. As she lifted the lid on a pan, a billow of steamy, fragrant sauerkraut blasted her in the face.

"What is that?" she cried. It not only reeked, there were white doughy lumps in the kraut.

Tiny looked her straight in the eye. "You wanted vegetables. Sauerkraut is supposed to improve digestion and help you lose weight. Course, the kniphla probably don't help much, but it tastes good. My neighbor brings some over when she makes a batch. Goes great with sausage."

With any other guy, she would have walked out the door and never looked back. However, this was Tiny. He stood watching for her reaction like a kid hoping his teacher likes his artwork. Her heart melted, even as her sense of smell went into emergency mode.

"You'll try it, won't you?"

"All right," she said slowly. She set the table and lit a couple candles while Tiny dished up the food. When they were seated, he offered his usual prayer. "God is great. God is good. Let us thank Him for this food. By his hands we all are fed. Give us, Lord, our daily bread. Amen."

Brianna put small amounts of food on her plate and daintily picked at the silky white pellets of dough. They actually tasted rather good doused in butter. Tiny lifted a forkful of sausage, kraut and kniphla to his mouth.

Still chewing, he said, "Tastes best eaten together." She mixed the three and had to agree.

As they ate, they talked about their changing lives. Brianna's truck would be ready in the next few days and the equipment for Tiny's Gym had arrived. He planned a soft opening over the weekend and a grand opening in January.

Toward the end of her meal, Brianna lifted her glass of water to Tiny and admitted, "You're a fairly good cook."

"I figured you'd like the kraut, but I wasn't sure about the deer sausage."

"Deer sausage?" Brianna set down her glass. "No! That's like eating Bambi. How could you let me do that?"

"Aw, do we have to go through this again? Sometimes you do animals a favor by harvesting them. I might have saved this deer from starving to death this winter. Not to mention, it's one more deer off the roads that won't cause an accident."

He had valid points, Brianna conceded. While she didn't want to think about them, she saw some truth in what he said.

"Let's not talk about it. Do you have something healthy for dessert?"

"Done," he said, jumping up from the table. "Close your eyes and wait here." He banged around in the kitchen for a few moments as Brianna sat with eyes innocently squeezed shut.

"Don't peek! What do you think it is?" he asked as he slid a plate in front of her.

"I smell chocolate. And marshmallow." She opened her eyes.

"Indoor S'mores," Tiny said eagerly. "I make them in the microwave."

"So much for healthy food," she murmured as she bit into melted chocolate and marshmallow squeezed between two graham crackers. "Mmm, this is delicious."

After the dishes were done, Tiny took her by the shoulders. "Bri, I want to take you shopping for an engagement ring of your dreams. I want everyone to know you're mine."

Brianna thought of how to respond. She knew Tiny didn't have a lot of extra cash, especially when he was opening a new business. Plus, her taste in jewelry was right up there with Princess Diana's. Besides, he had already given her a most romantic gift.

She fingered the pendant he'd given her for her birthday. A little research had revealed that it was yellow garnet. "What about this Mango Queen pendant? There is no diamond in the world that could mean half as much to me."

"You mean that?"

"With all of my heart. Let's get matching wedding bands instead." She paused. "What kind of wedding do you want?"

"I didn't hope to ever get married, so I haven't thought about it much. But I'd want all of my friends to come and help us celebrate." Tiny sat down on the couch, a big grin on his face. He leaned back and stretched his legs across half of the living room floor.

"Weddings are hazardous around here. Amber and Kelly got off easy. The only surprise they had was the buggy pulled by miniature horses. Oh yeah, and her brothers decorated their car with frosting and signs. Usually there are a lot more pranks."

Brianna was baffled. The weddings she attended had been elegant, formal, and rather stuffy affairs. "What kind of pranks?"

"Oh, the regular stuff, like stealing the bride, so the groom has to look for her. The worst case I heard was the groom's friends flew the bride to a different state and left her there." Tiny grinned at the astonishment in her eyes.

"If they know where the couple is staying on their wedding night, they mess up the room. One time, a couple was driving to catch a plane for their honeymoon and someone put Limburger cheese on the car's manifold. They smelled like cheese when they boarded the plane."

"What kind of friends would do that?" Brianna cried.

"Usually friends who've had a little red-eye or free beer."

"And what is red-eye?"

"It's an alcoholic drink that people make for celebrations."

"Like moonshine?"

"Hey, hey, never thought of it that way. Nah, it's more like they beef up a bottle of Everclear. For the record, I don't drink the stuff, but it's a tradition around here. Seen

a few fistfights at weddings, too, usually for the same reason."

"Not at my wedding!"

"I have a lot of friends in this town and everyone is
going to want to come. No matter what you say, there are
guys and gals who will cook up a little fun."

Brianna groaned. "Our wedding better not get rowdy!
It can be fun, but it's first a sacred time. We must also consider the parent factor. It's a stretch to think my parents
will come out here. And if Helena does get involved, she'll
want the wedding to happen in California."

"No California wedding. I'd be like a fish out of water.
Besides, it would make me feel funny to plan a big wedding
with your family when my mother is in the hospital."

"Yes, your mom. Should we try to see her? Do you
think she'll warm up to me?"

"Maybe we can make a trip to Jamestown before
Christmas. Take her a present and tell her the news." Tiny
seemed happy at the prospect.

"I don't know anyone else who has parent problems
like we do." Brianna moved over to the couch and snuggled next to Tiny. "What are we going to do?"

"The only thing we can do: ask the Good Lord for help."
Holding hands, they took turns pouring out their hopes,
dreams and anxieties in prayer. They asked God to help
them plan an exquisite (Brianna's word) and nice (Tiny's
word) ceremony, and closed with an earnest amen.

Then Tiny turned to her, his eyes sparkling. "I have an
idea."

# Chapter 25

# *The Trip*

The Saturday before Christmas, Brianna rose early. She and Tiny had a lot to accomplish. As the pale December sun rose, Brianna said a cheerful goodbye to Kate and Marge. Then she picked up her purse and a tote bag and rushed out the door to Tiny's waiting pickup.

"She told me not to wait up for her." Kate's voice quavered. "Can they have that much Christmas shopping to do?"

"It almost looks like they're eloping," Marge commented as she and Kate peeked out the front window.

Brianna had been up for hours and glammed up for the day with festive earrings, and a mini skirt and boots. She greeted Tiny with a brilliant smile and a quick kiss before fastening her seatbelt.

He looked her over and smiled in appreciation. "How did I get so lucky?"

"The feeling is mutual," she said. Tiny wore a new leather jacket and had tossed his green cap into the backseat. "This is going to be a wonderful day! A milestone for us."

"Yep. I'm glad both Rusty and June could work today. Together they can manage the Co-op without me. They're both level-headed, you know." That was a high compliment coming from Tiny.

"I brought breakfast." Brianna pulled a thermos out of her leather tote and poured coffee into two insulated mugs. "Have you ever had French pressed coffee?"

"Nope. I like strong coffee, like I make it at the Co-op. No wimpy French stuff for me."

"Well, at least try this." She took a sip of her own drink and savored the rich flavor for a few seconds.

Tiny lifted his mug to his lips, sipped and gulped. "Hey, hey, there's nothing wimpy about this coffee."

Brianna smiled and reached back into the tote. "If you approve of the coffee, maybe you'll find my homemade yogurt bars to your liking."

Tiny snorted. "That's crossing the line, Bri. I'm not eating none of that foo-foo stuff."

"I have two words for you: Deer. Sausage. If I can eat deer meat, it's only fair that you taste my blueberry yogurt bars. They're very nutritional."

"Blueberries and yogurt," Tiny groaned. "What's next? Kale cookies?"

"Just try the bar."

Tiny took a bite and began to chew. Brianna studied the road, waiting for his reaction. He took another bite. And another.

"Maybe we can make a deal," he finally said. "I'll try your food as long as you keep trying my food. Maybe it'll be good for both of us."

By the time the stores opened in downtown Bismarck, the couple was strolling along the sidewalk peeking in windows. The air remained calm but chilly, and they could see their breath. Christmas music played from a hidden loudspeaker. "Silver bells, silver bells," Brianna sang. "That's one of my favorite holiday songs."

They reached the quaint door of a jewelry store. A lovely chime rang as they went inside. The aroma of apple cider perking in a thirty-cup pot, colorful decorations and the quiet ticking of a dozen grandfather clocks added to the atmosphere.

They browsed the glass showcases, moving steadily in search of matching wedding bands. Tiny found them first. Then, looking back, he saw Brianna stop briefly at a group of diamond rings. He stepped over to her.

"Is there one you like?" he asked. "I know we talked about matching bands, but it's okay to change your mind."

"No, I love the idea of having matching bands."

Tiny pointed to a pear-shaped diamond. "Is that the one you like?"

"Yes, but I'm just looking. Honest. Where's the his-and-her section?"

Tiny glanced at the jeweler. "Can we see that one?"

"Certainly." He pulled the ring out and laid it on a black velvet background, where it caught the light.

"The pear is considered a 'fancy' diamond." He took a pen and pointed out the head, shoulders, belly and wings of the stone. "This isn't a large diamond, but it has high clarity, cut and color. Would you like to try it on?"

*Helping people pick out wedding bands must be a happy way to make a living*, Brianna thought as she slipped it on her finger. The ring fit perfectly.

"No." She shook her dark hair and pulled the ring off. It was certainly out of Tiny's price range, and they had already settled on what they wanted.

Moving on, she found the case with the matching rings, while behind her, Tiny and the jeweler exchanged glances.

"Do you like these?" she asked Tiny as she pointed to a set.

They tried on different bands until they settled on a set. The jeweler even found the right size for Tiny's large finger. They smiled at each other. They were really going to do this.

Just as the sale was being rung up, Brianna's phone interrupted the special moment. Pulling it from her purse, she groaned. "It's Jontel. I have to take this."

As she walked to the other side of the store for the business call, Tiny turned to the jeweler. "I'll take that pear-shaped diamond, as well as the set, if you will wrap the diamond separately so I can hide it from her."

"Certainly." The man smiled and discreetly pulled the ring from the case. He disappeared for several moments, returning with a small box wrapped in gold paper and a white ribbon. "That should fit in your pocket."

Once outside again, they held hands and hurried to the pickup. The second lap of their trip would take them to Jamestown. They spent their driving time discussing the rings before talk turned to the purpose of their visit. They were going to see Jolina, who was now able to receive visitors.

Realistically, Brianna should have hated the woman who had thrown birthday cake in her face. Yet, all she could feel was compassion for the fiery little woman.

The evening before she had questioned Tiny about Jolina's clothing. Had Tiny helped her pack a bag? Had the sheriff? Or was she carted off with no personal items? Tiny assured her that Jolina had what she needed, but Brianna wasn't so sure.

She had gone into Jolina's bedroom and looked around, noting the dismal clothes the woman owned. True, there was no sign of a toothbrush or hairbrush, and there were a few empty hangers in the closet. Maybe she had the minimum of what she needed. Still, she'd been hospitalized for weeks.

After some thought, she had put a few items in a bag, and then went into Jolina's workroom. Everything had remained as it was the day she'd been taken away, except for a growing layer of dust. She picked up a small doll that sat prominently on the sewing machine.

*Perhaps Jolina would like to see this friend,* she thought. Besides, what could she lose? The woman hated her, so if it upset her that Brianna had invaded her personal space, what did it matter? She placed the cover on the sewing machine so it wouldn't gather more dust and put the doll in the bag.

On the hundred-mile trip to Jamestown, she had convinced Tiny to stop at the mall and find some new clothing for Jolina for Christmas. In less than an hour, they had a new jogging suit, some T-shirts, pajamas and a bottle of hand lotion. Their final stop was a gift-wrapping station in the center of the mall.

"Ma never had a Christmas like this before," Tiny admitted. "She didn't like to celebrate much, and my dad thought it was a great day to get drunk. Since he died, we've kept it simple."

Brianna stared at him thoughtfully, wondering how he had become such a good man. She vowed to make up for all of his lost holidays.

"My Christmases were splashy. Gifts! Food! Parties! But they totally missed the real reason for the season," she said. "Speaking of food, what kind of candy does your mother like?" she asked as they strolled by a small candy store. They picked out a box of mixed chocolates. If she didn't like them, the other residents could eat them.

Brianna waited anxiously behind a mirrored window watching Tiny make his way through the visitor's room. Jolina sat shriveled and sedated at a table near the window. Other residents were engrossed in a television program. Tiny leaned over and hugged his mother. Then, he placed the box of candy in her hands and she smiled.

*Good start*, thought Brianna. Though she couldn't hear what they were saying, their faces and body language were positive. The meeting was going well. When he handed his mother a bright gift bag, her eyes lit up. She pulled the paper from the top and took out the pajamas and lotion. She hugged the pajamas to herself and then took the cap off the lotion and sniffed it.

They spent a few minutes together, and then Tiny nodded toward the window. Jolina got a quizzical look on her face and asked a question. Tiny took her petite hands in his and spoke earnestly to her.

Then he got up and came to the door. Brianna stood armed with a bag of Jolina's belongings and a box covered in red plaid paper with an enormous bow.

Brianna had completed oral college tests and modeled at fashion shows. She'd walked into meeting rooms armed with a portfolio and smoothly signed new clients. None of her experiences had intimidated her more than coming face to face with Jolina again.

Chapter 26

# Visit With Jolina

Brianna slowly walked toward the table where Jolina sat. "Hello, Mrs. Winger."

Jolina surveyed her clothes, hair and makeup. Brianna had seen that look before, usually when women were intimidated by her. In turn, Brianna studied the woman's face. Docile from drugs now, her eyes nonetheless had the wary look of an abused animal.

"She's tall," Jolina said to Tiny, never taking her eyes off Brianna.

Brianna slipped into a chair so she was at eye level. "I hope we can be friends."

"I want the best for my son," Jolina said, finally looking at her.

"I want the best for Tiny, too," Brianna said softly.

"What makes you think this woman is good enough?" Again, Jolina addressed Tiny.

Tears ran down Brianna's face and she reached for Jolina's small chapped hands. It was as if she could see into the older woman's soul, could see the despair of the past and the spark of life that burned somewhere within.

Jolina was willing to fight for her son, even from a position of complete weakness. This woman had moxie. *Would I be able to sit in a mental hospital with no earthly power and fight for someone I love?* Brianna wondered.

"I love Tiny, too. I'd never take him from you or hurt you in any way."

Was she really saying this to the woman who had plastered her with birthday cake and broken glass? And ruined her good coatdress. Yet, she felt an unconditional love for Jolina. Something like a power surge went through her body and a song hummed in her brain.

"May I call you Jolina?" she asked lightly.

The woman nodded.

"Jolina, do you remember the song that goes like this: It is no secret what God can do? What he's done for others, he'll do for you." Brianna's alto voice was soft with emotion.

Jolina paused for a moment, and then asked, "What's in the packages?"

Brianna sighed. "I brought some of your own things that you might need." She set the cloth bag on Jolina's lap.

She pulled out the little doll. "Sassy! Sassy!" she cried, surprising Brianna and Tiny, and gathering the attention of others in the room. "Where have you been? I've missed you."

A few minutes later, they said goodbye. As they glanced at her through the window in the hall, Jolina was tucking her doll under her arm. The other patients had gathered around her. Brianna felt sad for Jolina as she pushed the elevator button. Tiny was unusually quiet and they didn't speak on the way to the pickup.

Then, to her surprise, he laid his head on the steering wheel and sobbed. "I've never seen anything like what you did for Ma," he finally said. "How did you know she wanted that doll?"

"I didn't."

"Did you know that was her favorite song years back?"

"No way! Really? I didn't know. The song came to me while I was waiting to go in. Do you think God can put thoughts in your head?" Brianna wondered aloud.

After pondering the visit for a few more calming minutes, they were ready to leave for Cottonwood Creek. They took the shortcut via U.S. Highway 52 and N.D. Highway 200.

As they drove through Jamestown, Brianna noted it was a pretty town set in a river valley and filled with towering trees. Their route took them past a couple large churches, through the business district and then up out of the valley past a lake. Soon, they were out in the open prairie that was becoming so familiar to her.

Tiny suggested they stop at a popular restaurant along the way for a late lunch. Brianna agreed. Her breakfast bar was long past staving off hunger. Once seated, she almost jumped up and did a cartwheel when she found fresh salmon on the menu. *Who knew you could find fresh salmon in the hinterlands?* she wondered.

"Tell me more about your mother," Brianna said as they waited for their meal.

"Bri, she'll get out of the hospital and be kind of normal, but sooner or later she'll get off her meds. It's a cycle with her. Try not to get too hopeful."

"There has to be a way to break the cycle," she murmured. Jolina needed another woman in her life and Brianna decided to make a special point of seeing to her needs.

"You still want to marry me? After meeting Ma?"

"Of course. After all, you haven't met my mother yet. Besides, we have wedding rings!

Brianna paused for a moment. "I wonder if we need our birth certificates to get a marriage license? That could be a problem. We moved so many times, I'm not sure my mother kept a copy. Besides, I haven't heard from her for months."

"We may not need them," Tiny offered. "If we do, mine is in a box of documents and photos. Let's go home and look. There might be more information about Ma in the box."

A couple hours later, they sat at the dining room table with a metal box open in front of them. Tiny began going through each paper and envelope. However, Brianna noticed he slipped something out of the box and sat on it.

"Here's a couple of pictures of Ma when she was in high school. She was an Air Force brat. Her old man transferred to Minot and that's where she met my dad, who was a local boy."

"What happened?"

"Shotgun wedding. Her folks didn't like Dad at all. I don't know the whole story, but I never met any grandparents. Don't know where they live or if they're even alive."

"That's a sad story. What was your mother's maiden name?"

"Jolina Monroe." He pulled out a black and white photo, studied it and turned it over. "What the heck. It says, 'The Monroes. 1956. Micah, Betty, Jolina 6 months.'"

He handed the photo to Brianna. A happy young couple smiled back at her. The woman had long blonde hair and wore a sundress. The man had a crewcut and wore a military uniform. The woman held a baby in a ruffled bonnet and knit booties.

"You inherited your grandmother's blonde hair," she said as she returned the photo. "Do you have any other photos of Jolina or your dad?"

When Tiny went in search of a photo album in Jolina's workroom, Brianna spied the envelope he'd slid under his seat. Opening it, she found his birth certificate. She quickly read his vital statistics and then clapped her hands over her mouth. She snorted in surprise just as Tiny came back into the room.

"Give me that!"

"No." She stood and held the birth certificate behind her back. "Is that your real name?"

"Nope. Well, maybe. Just give it here." His easy-going manner was gone.

Brianna relented and handed him the birth certificate. "It's okay." She wrapped her arms around his neck. "You can trust me."

"This can never get out," he said firmly. "In fact, maybe we should get married in another county so nobody at the courthouse sees this."

Brianna was still smiling over her newfound information about Tiny when he dropped her off at home. Everyone was in bed, but Kate had left a lamp on in the front entry. As Brianna went to shut it off, she saw a package addressed to her on the table. It was filled with postmarks and stamps, and the return address was in England. *It has to be from Daddy*, she thought, as she flicked off the light and scampered upstairs with her find.

The package contained a phone card, a book of poetry and a typewritten letter. She unfolded the letter.

*My Dearest Briannie Bee,*
*This letter will arrive long after your birthday, but with the help of the English and American postal services, should reach you before Christmas. Please know that I thought of you every hour on your birthday. I'm so proud of the young woman you have become (tho I'd like to see you again in a ponytail and braces as you were at age ten.)*

*Can you forgive me for not keeping in touch? As you probably know, Helena moved back to the States. No doubt she's given you the story, so I'll spare you the details of the upheaval, except to say I tried to convince her to stay and considered resigning my job to go back with her.*

*In the end, I stayed here because my work project is most crucial. I have a little house in the suburbs, where it's quite peaceful. I go for runs on the weekend and en-*

*joy reading before the fire. You will be surprised that I've been attending a little brick church near here.*

*I hope you've found a place to call home and that you're among friends. Please let me know how you are and consider coming to see me. I'm sending a phone card so you can call when it's convenient for you. I'm also passing on a little volume of psalms that I've enjoyed.*

*Your Daddy,*

*Eldon Davis*

Brianna had forgotten his pet name for her. Now she was crying long before she read the last line. Her Daddy had written and called her by the name he used when she was little. He missed her and knew intuitively that she needed a place to put down roots. She was thankful that he explained what had happened much more fully than her mother had. And he was going to church. She couldn't wait to tell Kelly that.

Sighing, she wiped away her tears and hugged the letter to her chest. The world had just become a happier place.

# Chapter 27

# Christmas Surprise

Another nightmare awakened Brianna on Christmas Eve morning. Fear forced her to turn on the lamp and peer into the shadows, but there was no one in the room.

There wasn't much use in trying to go back to sleep, so Brianna showered and dressed. Soon she sat at the dining room table nursing her coffee and staring at a piece of cherry kuchen.

In the kitchen, Marge rattled around as she packed boxes of cookies and candy to take on a trip to see their kids. Brianna would miss Marge and Wayne, who were leaving for a month. Still, she looked forward to a quiet Christmas.

Putting thoughts of the nightmare aside, she counted the many positive things going on in her life. She fingered a letter from her father that she carried in her pocket, relieved that she could finally tell Tiny and Kate that she'd heard from him.

Then, she smiled at the thought of Tiny's real name. After she found his birth certificate, he'd stumbled to explain that his parents had argued over his name, so his mother spitefully chose a name and put it on the birth certificate. *Fun couple*, she thought.

Along with the birth certificate, they found info about Jolina's father. Micah Monroe was an officer in the Air Force and the family had moved from Minot after she married. Brianna wondered if Tiny's grandparents were still living. Would they want to see Jolina or meet Tiny? Finding the family might bring healing for Jolina and for Tiny.

Brianna glanced out the window. A light snow had fallen during the night and now sparkled like diamonds in the pale light of dawn. Diamonds. Tiny didn't know it, but Brianna watched him purchase the pear-shaped diamond ring. She should have stopped his extravagance, but it was such a beautiful act of love that she couldn't bear to object.

She had her own wow-factor gift planned for Tiny. He'd been too busy at the Co-op and opening the gym, to inquire about the old Johnson gas station, the decrepit building on Main Street. The one that Tiny gawked at whenever he drove up Main Street. The one with so many possibilities.

She wanted to buy it, but could she afford it? Maybe. Real estate in Cottonwood City was a fraction of what it was in California. Monday morning, she planned to make some contacts. The idea of buying it for Tiny warmed her heart. It could be the next step for their Dream Team.

Brianna eyed the cherry kuchen. She was reaping the consequences of Marge's good baking. When she'd tried on her mango dress recently, she couldn't zip it up.

Still, she bit into the kuchen. Her mother would never know she'd gained a couple pounds. Or as Tiny put it in his unvarnished way, she was putting some meat on her bones.

They needed to pick a wedding date. Thoughts of marrying during the holidays had been quashed. Now, they were considering a smallish wedding on Valentine's Day or a bigger wedding in the summer.

Kate appeared in the doorway just then. "My, you came home late and got up early." She cocked her head. "I thought you'd sleep in today. I hope you didn't have another nightmare. 'Twas you moving around upstairs before dawn wasn't it?"

Brianna nodded, her happy thoughts fleeing through the back door of her mind. The memory of the nightmare made her shudder. She needed to find out what was causing them.

"Well, I'm going to pray that they go away. You should be having sweet dreams, especially when you spent all day with your fiancé."

Brianna gave the older woman a knowing smile. Kate wanted details. "We had a wonderful day. Picked out wedding bands and visited Jolina."

"Do tell." Kate lowered her ample body into a chair across the table. "Was she civil?"

"It went fine. We stopped and bought Christmas gifts for her, and I took some things that I thought she might miss. Tiny went in first and prepared her. Kate, I think the problem is less about me and more that she wants to protect Tiny."

"She had a hard life, and Tiny is her only son."

"Did you know she makes dolls?"

"I don't know much about her at all. She was always secretive." Kate glanced at her watch. "We need to leave if we don't want to be late for church."


The next couple of days were a blur of phone calls and meetings.

She'd placed an ad for her Miata in the Bismarck Tribune, and it sold. She cleaned out the glove compartment, and waved goodbye to her "jelly bean" as the new owner sped off in her faithful travel partner.

It was like watching her former life drive off into the setting sun. Now, the refurbished milk truck sat in front of the house, a symbol of the future. The new paint was stunning, the detailing perfect, and the tires were worthy of winter roads.

"Oh my," Kate crowed from the front porch. "How did you ever get Davis Designs written on the side like that?"

"It's called an advertising wrap. Do you like it?"

"I think everyone will want to hire you when they see your truck."

She had made several contacts about the Johnson gas station. The owner wanted to sell the property and he had named a price she could live with. She felt confident the sale would go through.

So did Sam Smith. The banker gave her the key to the building so they could walk through and take a more thorough look. Now, she put the key in a little box for Tiny and wrapped it in some of Kate's recycled Christmas paper.

Kate, Tiny and Brianna planned to attend the Christmas Eve candlelight service and then come back to Schulteville for dinner. The menu was mouthwatering. Night Before Christmas Clam Chowder, followed by a pheasant and wild rice dish prepared by Tiny. Brianna would make a salad of mixed greens, dried cranberries and pecans. Kate's favorite holiday dessert, bread pudding with raisins, was in the fridge.

On Christmas Day, they would have a leisurely brunch and spend the rest of the day opening gifts, playing board games, and watching college football on television. She looked forward to the peaceful, intimate time.

On Christmas Eve, the table was set with the good china, crystal and silver on a hand-embroidered tablecloth. When Tiny saw the elegant setting, Brianna had to convince him in a whispered conference that he wouldn't break anything.

"Put your napkin on your lap right away," she advised, "and as for all that silverware? Use the outside pieces first or just follow my lead." She squeezed his calloused hand.

Soon they were seated at the table, dipping their soup spoons into chowder. Tiny was just stabbing into the basket of fragrant rolls with his fork when they heard car doors slam. When the doorbell rang, Brianna sighed, Kate shrugged, and Tiny put his fork down.

"Santa Claus?" Tiny asked hopefully.

"Carolers," Kate surmised.

Brianna strolled through the parlor on her way to answer the door, noting that the Queen Anne house brimmed with holiday décor. She had lugged boxes of vintage decorations downstairs. Wayne dug out a faded artificial Christmas tree, which she dressed up with reflector lights, antique balls, and silver tinsel.

Brianna adjusted her turtleneck sweater, put on a smile and opened the door, expecting carolers or a neighbor delivering a plate of cookies.

"Helena! Uncle Fab? What are you doing here?"

Helena pushed her way into the house, grabbed Brianna's hands and air-kissed her cheeks. "I just had to spend Christmas with my darling daughter," she exclaimed.

"We hope you have room for us at the inn," Uncle Fab chimed in as he shut the door.

Brianna's back muscles tensed. "I can't believe you're here. Why didn't you call?"

"Well, that's some greeting. We took two flights, rented a car, and drove for miles through the dark to surprise you."

Brianna heard a sound behind her and turned. Kate held her chin high, a Mack truck in a yellow and red knit Christmas sweater. Her cane somehow resembled a weapon as she appraised the newcomers. Tiny stood with his arms crossed over his chest, a wary look on his face.

"Kate, meet my mother, Helena Davis, and my Uncle Fab." Kate gave a frosty smile. "Kate Schulte is my business partner and mentor. And this is her beautiful home." Then she linked her arm with Tiny's. "And this is my fiancé, Tiny Winger."

"Fiancé?" Helena's eyes swept over Tiny as she evaluated her daughter's choice. "That's an odd name. What is your given name?"

Before Tiny could answer, Kate stepped in. "Of course you're welcome to stay. Our guest rooms aren't all redecorated yet, but they're comfortable."

"Thank you." Helena sounded relieved. *Perhaps she realizes that they shouldn't have just barged in,* Brianna thought.

"Congratulations, Tiny, you picked a thoroughbred," Uncle Fab said with a wink. Uncle Fab sniffed the air, which was filled with the aroma of good food.

There was an awkward silence before her mother began prattling on. "What a difficult trip. By the time we left the airport in Bismarck, we were simply starved. We looked for a good restaurant, but there was nothing open. Before we knew it, we were driving out of the town. I thought we'd driven off the edge of the earth."

"We were just sitting down to dinner. You must join us," Kate offered.

"Thank you," Fab said. "I say, Tiny, will you help me bring in the bags?"

"Sure thing." When Tiny stepped forward, Uncle Fab handed him the car keys.

"Four bags. I'll open the door when you bring them in. I hate this cold weather."

Brianna frowned at the way Uncle Fab treated Tiny.

Kate placed a calming hand on her arm. "Let's put down some extra place settings, Brianna, and reheat the food."

Brianna sighed and paused for a moment before politely telling her mother, "Helena, the powder room is through that door if you wish to freshen up. I'll show you to your rooms later."

She needed a few minutes in the kitchen to adjust to the intrusion into their peaceful holiday. She would make the best of it. After all, Helena and Uncle Fab had traveled a long way to spend Christmas with her. She should be thrilled. Right?

A few minutes later, she came into the dining room with the pheasant dish. Kate had added extra place settings and was seated at the table with Tiny and Helena.

Uncle Fab had set up a large portable bar on the buffet and was chatting as he mixed a drink. "Here's to Christmas!" he exclaimed as he held up his glass.

Kate's lips were pursed and her eyes dark with fury. She considered alcohol to be the devil's brew. And, now it was being served in her own dining room.

# It Came Upon a Midnight Clear

Christmas Eve dinner didn't resume until after ten that evening. The merry evening had collapsed into an awkward social event, reminding Brianna of how much she hated her mother's idea of fun.

Before they could begin, Uncle Fab and Helena enjoyed a cocktail or two and talked about the gala they had attended earlier that week while the meal grew cold again.

When they proceeded to finish off a bottle of wine during the meal, Brianna suspected Kate was more than peeved. She sat rigidly and picked at her food. *Kate's tongue must be bleeding from biting it,* she thought.

Tiny was quiet as he kept an eye on which fork Brianna was using. Her mind whirled with the fact that her family had shown up. She had to admit that her mother was still beautiful at fifty. Her high cheekbones, perfectly coifed hair and flawless makeup still caused a stir wherever she went. Uncle Fab looked dapper in his tweed jacket, bow tie and flashy gold rings.

Their arrival also threw her into the role of waitress. Kate couldn't manage her cane and carry dishes between the dining room and kitchen, and Tiny was as much a guest as her family. She found new appreciation for Marge's adeptness in making pleasant and delicious meals.

When they were finally finished, Tiny helped Brianna remove the dishes. Tiny perked some coffee for everyone.

Together they delivered dessert plates of warm bread pudding smothered in caramel sauce.

During the meal that seemed to never end, the brother and sister gave colorful accounts of their long day of travel. Brianna had made similar trips several times, but hadn't mentioned the details to anyone. She wouldn't have considered making a big deal out of taking a 737 to Denver and then walking to the very end of the airport to catch a commuter flight into Bismarck.

"This dessert is simply marvelous, Mrs. Schulte. I do hope you will share the recipe," Helena complimented at the end of the meal.

"It's *Miss* Schulte." Kate's voice was clipped. "You may call me Kate. However, the recipe isn't mine to give away. It belongs to our wonderful housekeeper, Marge Selby. I'm afraid you won't see her, though. She and her husband Wayne are on a well-deserved vacation."

While Brianna and Tiny cringed at the rebuke, Helena hardly noticed. "Brianna and I only allow ourselves to indulge like this on holidays, don't we Brianna? Day after tomorrow, it's back on the diet."

Then she frowned. "I hope you're still watching your weight, Darling. You look rather robust. And so do you, Tiny."

Before anyone could respond, Uncle Fab got up and found a bottle of brandy in his mini bar. When he offered to pour a shot in each person's cup of coffee, Kate let out a yelp and put her hands over her cup. Then she stood abruptly and announced that she was going to bed. With a few quiet instructions to Brianna, she turned and clumped out of the room.

"You must be exhausted, also," Brianna said to the guests as she stood. "I'll show you to your rooms. I'm sure you'll find them to your liking."

Tiny hauled all of the suitcases upstairs, while Brianna showed Helena the best room in the house. Martha's Room was the only one that had been redecorated, and Helena gushed over the spacious accommodations.

"Mom, I mean Helena...," Brianna paused. She had burning questions, such as why had they suddenly appeared and where was her father? However, she realized she didn't have enough energy to probe her mother. The questions could wait until tomorrow.

Too late, Brianna realized she'd have to share the Jack and Jill bath with her uncle. She discreetly removed her personal items to her room.

While Tiny headed down the stairs, Uncle Fab grabbed her hand. "You've grown up to be such a beautiful young woman. Why, it seems like only yesterday that I used to tuck you in."

"That was a long, long time ago," Brianna murmured as she pulled away. Then she went back downstairs and embraced Tiny in the light of the Christmas tree. The colored bulbs gave a special glow to the room and the grandfather clock chimed the half-hour as they stood quietly.

"I never dreamed they would show up for Christmas," she whispered into his chest. "Did they scare you much?"

"Some. But, I can see more of what your life was like. Are you sure you want to leave their fancy way of life?"

"You mean am I sure I want to *escape* my old life?"

"Well, when you put it that way."

"I love you."

Tiny looked into her eyes for several moments. "I love you, too."

"I'm too wound up to go to sleep yet, come help me in the kitchen," she said as she pulled him along.

Dirty dishes and pans lined every countertop. Brianna made a sweeping motion with her hands. "Every one of these dishes, glasses and silverware has to be washed and dried by hand. I never want to own anything so labor-intensive. Life is too short to worry about keeping up appearances."

"Maybe we can do the dishes and then snuggle awhile?" Tiny asked as he grabbed a dishtowel from a stack. "If you wash and I dry, it won't take long."

The kitchen seemed like a private world in the middle of the night, and they talked about many things as they began with the silverware and glasses. When a crystal goblet slipped through Tiny's fingers and crashed to the floor, they both looked at it with dismay.

"Kate's gonna kill me," Tiny moaned.

"That reminds me. I still haven't replaced the plate that Jolina threw at me. We're hard on dishes. When we get married, maybe we should get plastic dishes and glasses."

"And plastic silverware," Tiny offered, and they both started snickering.

Within an hour, the gleaming dinnerware stood ready to be put away in the morning. Tomorrow, Brianna determined, they would use a dishwasher-friendly set of dishes.

"Will you open your gift tonight while we're alone?" she asked, leading him to the parlor.

"That sounds great. You should open yours, too."

They sat on the Oriental rug by the tree and traded small boxes.

"You first," Tiny said. Brianna slowly undid the elegant wrapping, pledging to keep the ribbon as a keepsake. She opened the box to find the pear-shaped diamond ring.

"It's the one from the jewelry store."

She put on the ring and held out her hand. It reflected a rainbow of colors as it caught the lights from the tree.

"I thought the Mango Queen ought to have a ring that is just as fine as she is. I could see you liked it a lot."

"I adore this ring. It's the best gift I've ever received, next to this." She pulled out the necklace Tiny had given her for her birthday.

Tiny beamed, showing the space between his front teeth. She admired the ring a bit more and then urged Tiny to open his gift. He looked confused when he opened the box and saw a key.

"It's the key to the Johnson gas station. I'm in the process of buying the building for us. For you. For the Brianna and Tiny Dream Team. I'm sorry the deal isn't finished yet, but it's looking good and the banker let me have the key so we can inspect the building more closely."

Tiny was quiet for several moments before asking, "You're buying the Johnson place?"

"Yes, but it will be our place, not just my place."

"That's mindboggling." He hugged her then and gave her a long, slow kiss.

Then, Kate's voice called out, "Will you two break it up? It's the middle of the night!"

Her voice shocked them into silence before they began to laugh as quietly as possible. Then Tiny sighed, "I better go. Morning will be here before we know it."

After a quick goodnight at the door, Brianna watched Tiny drive off. She fingered the diamond on her left hand as she unplugged the Christmas lights and tiptoed upstairs. If they'd decided to marry on Christmas Eve, he wouldn't be driving away now.

And she was convinced that she was making the right choice in staying here to make a new life with him.

# Chapter 29

# Christmas Morning

When Brianna slipped downstairs on Christmas morning, Kate beckoned her into her room. She went in, shut the door behind her and sat cross-legged on the bed.

"Brianna, have you heard the term "Seize the Day?"

"Carpe diem. Make the most of the present moment."

"Yes, that's it. Your mother and uncle took me off guard last night and I'm sorry I didn't react more kindly. Now I think we must make the most of the time they're here. Let's show them some North Dakota hospitality and show them what Christmas means to us. Plus, did you know that God is providing a real winter wonderland?" Kate added slyly.

Brianna frowned, then scrambled across the bed and drew back the curtain. Snow fell in big lazy flakes covering the town in the pale morning light.

"Oh, it's beautiful. And you're right. This year I'm really seeing the true meaning of Christmas, and I would love to share that with them."

They spent a few minutes making plans for the day. Then, leaving Kate to make phone calls, Brianna got dressed and knocked on the bedroom doors as she went down the hall. "Merry Christmas! Meet us in the parlor in one hour."

Fab startled her by throwing open his door. "How do I look?" he asked, modeling a red bowtie and his tweed jacket.

"You look great."

He lifted one hand in a mock toast and grasped her arm with the other.

*Time to seize the day*, she thought. "I need to talk to you and I'll get right to the point," she whispered as she pried his hand from her arm. "This is Kate's house and she doesn't approve of alcohol. Do me a favor and be a good guest. Forget about drinking today."

"What do you mean? It's a holiday."

Brianna folded her arms and tapped her foot, as she waited for a better answer. She was an inch taller than her uncle was and used her height as an advantage, looking directly in his eyes.

"Well, maybe as a favor to my favorite niece," he finally answered with a wink.

"I trust that you mean that," Brianna said with a snarky smile and then bolted downstairs to finish preparations.

It seemed like only a few minutes until Tiny arrived with a load of plastic grocery bags hung on his arm. "Presents for your family," he said as he shrugged out of his green parka.

When he spied Helena and Fab coming down the stairs, his eyes grew big. Helena was tall, with long dark hair, and wore a silky white pantsuit with a leopard print scarf and matching mules. This older version of Brianna seemed to befuddle him, and he glanced down at his plaid flannel shirt and sighed.

"You look fine," Brianna whispered. "I'm wearing plaid, too." She adjusted the red and green plaid wool pashmina she'd selected to go over her black slacks and sweater.

"Say, is that breakfast I smell?" Uncle Fab asked loudly.

Soon they sat down for an informal brunch using dishes that Brianna could put in the dishwasher. The table was loaded with an egg casserole Marge had left in the fridge for them, plus sausage, citrus fruit and cherry and peach kuchen. Brianna wondered if her mother would like the sausage Tiny brought.

From the start, Kate took command of the table talk. "I'm afraid we didn't give you our best welcome last night. I apologize. We want to make that up to you by sharing our way of life with you during the rest of your stay."

Brianna added, "There are gifts to open and a special surprise for you later in the day, but after brunch we'll make a special time to remember the reason for this season."

Then, Kate began sharing her family's story. Brianna imagined she was rehearsing for the day she would regale paying guests at the bed and breakfast. "You probably wonder how my family came to live in the heart of Dakota," Kate began.

Brianna doubted the question had crossed their minds.

"My parents bought land here in about 1900. They worked very hard and by 1913, they were able to build this house. Then, my father realized he'd built a beautiful house for his wife, but there was no church in town. So he donated the land and helped build the little church across the street. Then my brother, Ted, and I were born. Ted was pastor of the church for sixty years!"

Kate swallowed quickly and looked down at her plate for several moments, while Brianna explained, "Ted died last year."

"What an interesting story," Uncle Fab exclaimed. "I saw that little building, but it didn't look like a church."

"It isn't a church anymore," Kate answered as she dabbed at her eyes with a white hanky. "Now we attend Cottonwood Church, where Kelly Jorgenson is the pastor. Perhaps you'll stay long enough to go with us on Sunday."

Helena shifted in her chair. "We can only stay a couple days. We have social obligations at home."

"That's a shame," Kate crowed. "There is so much we want to show you about our wonderful Cottonwood Creek community."

Fab's eyes roamed the room, no doubt searching for his portable bar. Brianna and Tiny had shoved it into the kitchen pantry last night. Finally, he eyed the platters of food on the table. "Say, can you pass me some more of that sausage?"

"It is quite flavorful," Helena commented. "What brand is it?"

"That's a buck I shot at the slough east of town a few weeks ago," Tiny said with pride.

Helena laid down her fork and pushed her plate away.

Kate doggedly continued her story. "Wayne Selby moved his carpentry business into the church earlier this year. He builds church furnishings that ship all over the nation."

"I spend a lot of time in the carpentry shop, too," Brianna said.

Helena looked blankly at her daughter. "Whatever for? I thought you were working remotely for that design firm in San Francisco."

"I still work with Jontel, but I have a start-up company, Davis Designs."

"I say, Davis Designs is a wonderful name. What do you design?" Uncle Fab asked.

"I'm doing interior decorating. My first job was to do Amber Jorgenson's new insurance office last month. I'm also renovating this house to be a bed and breakfast."

"She and Amber decorated my gym, too. It's real classy," Tiny added.

"Your work in San Francisco is such a well-paying job," Helena commented. "May I ask if you're making any money with Davis Designs?"

"I will. Of course, I didn't charge Amber because we're good friends and we did the work together." She wrapped her arm around Tiny's. "Tiny doesn't have to pay because

Amber and I put in new flooring and painted the walls before he could say anything. It's been good advertising."

Her mother froze when Brianna mentioned doing manual labor. Uncle Fab fiddled with his bow tie.

"I also make signs."

"What kind of signs?" Helena asked with disdain.

"You'll have to wait and see," Brianna said as she picked up her juice glass.

Kate sucked in her breath. "What are you wearing on your finger?" The others turned their attention to Brianna's left hand. She put the glass down and held up her hand for all to see.

"An engagement ring." She meant to smile. Instead, tears filled her eyes and her lower lip trembled.

Tiny looked dismayed.

"Don't worry, Tiny, I'm really happy." Tears rolled down her cheeks. "The ring is so special and we're going to get married and my family, except for Daddy, is here. It's a wonderful Christmas."

Tiny sighed and said, "I guess I have a lot to learn about women." He drew sympathetic laughter.

"Speaking of your marriage," Helena said. "We just attended the most beautiful ceremony. One of your high school classmates. An eligible bachelor. Assistant state's attorney. The wedding took place overlooking the Pacific with a string quartet playing."

"And a champagne fountain," Uncle Fab added.

"I want your wedding to be something like that, but we must begin planning right away. You know how long it takes to get a good venue." Helena spoke to Brianna, but she was eyeing Tiny, as though evaluating how he would do at one of her soirees.

Brianna responded with a simple solution. "We don't need a venue because we already have one. We plan to get married at Cottonwood Church."

"Oh no, absolutely not! I've been waiting all my life to plan this wedding. It'll be the event of the year. Think, Brianna, all of your friends will just die if they aren't invited."

Tiny looked stricken.

"I haven't lived there for years. I doubt anyone will care," Brianna countered.

Tiny let out an audible sigh.

"Well, I care and I insist that you come home to be married." Helena's words were as strong and polished as stainless steel.

Tension built as everyone waited for Brianna's response. The muscles in her neck were so tight that her hair follicles hurt. She looked at Kate, whose face clearly said, "not now."

Tiny cleared his throat. "Hey, it's Christmas Day. I move that we talk about the wedding another time."

"I second that," Kate spoke up.

"Meeting adjourned," Tiny quickly responded.

Brianna briefly wondered where that came from and then remembered Tiny attended monthly Co-op board meetings. She squeezed his hand.

"I think the sausage would pair well with a good stout beer," Uncle Fab offered helpfully.

And with that, Christmas brunch ground to an end.

Chapter 30

# Heart to Heart with Helena

By the time Christmas brunch was over, the snow had stopped falling. Tiny put on his parka and went out to sweep off the steps and shovel the sidewalk.

Kate strolled into the parlor with Uncle Fab, while Brianna and Helena began stacking dishes and taking them to the kitchen. When Brianna went back to the dining room for the remaining tableware, she couldn't help but eavesdrop on Kate and Fab's conversation.

"Fab is an interesting name," Kate commented. "Is that your Christian name or a nickname?"

"My name is Fabian Demetri Mond. We're European, you know. I've always been called Fab, like the laundry soap. I took a teasing when I was a boy. Since Brianna was born, I've been Uncle Fab. I like that better."

"So what do you do for a living?"

"I've dabbled in several ventures."

*He's a good dabbler and a charmer,* Brianna thought. Offhand, she couldn't remember any job he held for long, perhaps because he saw himself as a moneyed gentleman, above doing actual work. She'd always accepted his genial ways and social drinking, but they didn't sit well with her anymore.

She listened to their conversation for a few moments, and then instead of returning to the kitchen, she hurried upstairs to her room and closed the door. Taking a deep breath, she looked out the window at the quiet snowy scene and then turned and spied her wall hanging.

Why did the light always seem to shine on that one certain line? "A garment of praise instead of a spirit of despair."

"Lord, I need you," she said, as she dropped to her knees. For a moment, she imagined God up in heaven, far above the little village. From his vantage point, it must look like a toy town. In the width and breadth of eternity, their human arguments must look foolish. Her muscles began to relax.

A few moments later, she opened the door to the bathroom, planning to splash water on her face. Fab had all but taken over the tiny bathroom, hanging his dripping towel alongside hers and leaving clothes on the floor. Opening the medicine cabinet, she found he'd placed several items in it, including two kinds of aftershave.

She decided to check them out. One was his regular scent, but the other had a cloying musky smell. *That's creepy*, she thought. *It smells like the aftershave in my dream.* With a shudder, she clapped the cover on again and shut the medicine cabinet. With her mother waiting for her downstairs, she'd have to deliberate about this later.

When she ducked back into the kitchen, Helena was already refrigerating the leftovers. Brianna had to admit that with all her experience with entertaining, Helena could really whip around the kitchen.

She longed to have a heart-to-heart talk with her mother as they worked together. *Isn't that what a lot of women do?* However, Helena's usual idea of a mother-daughter talk was to correct Brianna and organize her life for her.

For certain, becoming a Christian and marrying Tiny were not in Helena's plans. Would her mother accept her choices? Still, this was a rare opportunity to try to make her understand.

"Thanks for helping," Brianna said. "I hoped we could have some time alone."

Helena turned and looked directly at her. "Yes. We should talk about the wedding."

"We should, but not today. There are some other things to discuss. Such as, I want to know about Daddy. Why did you leave him in England?"

"I'm very happy to be back in California and he's happy in dreary old England. Haven't you heard from him?" Helena asked as she wiped off the kitchen table.

"He sent a letter recently, but I wanted to hear what you have to say. You really didn't tell me much. Are you... do you plan to divorce?"

"What a thing to ask, especially when you won't talk about your own upcoming marriage. No. We're not planning to divorce. Yet. However, if he insists on living six thousand miles away, we're bound to drift further apart."

Brianna stared at her mother for a minute and then looked away. She wanted to find comfort in the fact that Helena was back in the states. However, the idea that she came back alone was unsettling.

"There's something else. I want to know why you and Uncle Fab showed up here unannounced." *And uninvited.*

Her mother was the poster girl for wrinkle-free skin. Helena refused to frown, squint or smile, so she wouldn't cause extra lines on her face. Brianna watched for nuances in her eyes and voice.

A bad-puppy look in her eyes gave away her guilt. "We came to insist that you come home. We thought hillbillies had kidnapped you."

"Hillbillies?" Dismay ran through Brianna. She imagined Helena and Fab sitting under a palm tree in their backyard sipping martinis and discussing how to rescue her.

*Did they have it wrong*, she thought resentfully. Then, a smile lit up her face. Tiny drove a pickup and lived in a mobile home. All he needed was a coonhound to complete the stereotype.

At least her mother was truthful, even if her ideas were insulting. It wouldn't hurt to be truthful about her own first trip to the state.

"You know, the first time I came out here with Kelly's parents, I had an attitude, too. I didn't see the goodness of the people or the beauty of the land. I hope you give it all a chance. Really look at your surroundings and allow yourself to be better acquainted with Tiny and Kate."

Helena touched a crystal glass that sat on the counter. "So far, it isn't at all like I pictured. Kate's family must have had some status here."

"*Kate* has status because she was superintendent of schools for decades. And she's a woman of influence for many other reasons." She bit her lip. Did she sound defensive?

"Don't bite your lip, Brianna. It makes you look anxious." Her expression showed that she was not aware of how her words affected her daughter. "And Tiny. What is his given name anyhow? Is he a person of status?"

Brianna bent over the dishwasher. Was that all the woman could think about? She took a couple deep breaths and said a quick prayer for help. Then she stood up and said matter-of-factly, "Tiny is an influencer."

"What does that mean?"

"He isn't wealthy and he wouldn't make your list of social contacts. However, he has his finger on the pulse of the community. He knows everyone. Makes things happen. I hear the teens in the youth group adore him."

Helena had been systematically cleaning the counters as they talked. Now she stopped and asked, "What does he do for a living?"

"He manages the Co-op." Brianna had learned that the people in the community owned the cooperative. She doubted her mother would understand the need or the idea.

"Is he able to give you the kind of life you're accustomed to?"

Brianna looked at the ceiling, hoping for some help from above. Then she sighed. "I hope not! My ideas and dreams have changed so much. You talked about being in the Denver airport. Did you know I was stranded there for thirty-six hours during a snowstorm last Christmas?"

"That's appalling!"

"Actually, the storm was a blessing. You see, even though my career was going great, I was miserable. You and Daddy moved away and Jontel left for Sweden, so I felt totally alone. I decided to fly out here to see Kelly. Whatever he and Kyle had, I knew I needed it, too."

"Kyle. He was such a nice boy, although he was so... religious," Helena interjected. "I know how it broke your heart when he was killed."

*Is that sympathy coming from my mother?* "We might have married someday if he had lived," Brianna whispered. "But I think he'd be happy for me now. Both Kyle and Kelly encouraged me to ask Jesus to come into my life. So, I did it."

"Oh, so this is about being a Christian?" Helena didn't try to mask her contempt.

"Yes. A wonderful thing happened to me! My situation didn't change that moment in Denver, but the heaviness lifted from my heart."

"Brianna, you're a strong, talented woman. You don't need a religious crutch."

"A crutch?" Brianna felt offended for a moment but regained her composure. "Not a crutch, it's more like a friendship. It's hard to explain the deep bond you can have with God, but it's so real."

She brought out containers of fudge, cookies, and nuts. Helena sat at the table and began helping her fill decorative plates for later.

"Since then, Amber and the others have become the best friends I've ever had. So, when Amber had that car accident in August, I wanted to be here to help her. Then Tiny picked me up at the airport in Bismarck, and that was the beginning of our relationship." She opened a jug of apple cider, poured it into a large coffee pot and plugged it in.

"Brianna, you've had many good friends. Every time we moved you made friends," Helena pointed out.

"Where are they now? They were there for a moment and then they disappeared." She studied her mother, and then her voice dropped with realization. "I bet you haven't had many real friends, either."

Helena jumped from her chair. "That's absurd! You know how many friends I have."

The conversation ended when Tiny peeked around the kitchen door. He apologized for interrupting, and then said Kate wanted to see them in the parlor.

*A divine interruption*, Brianna decided. She'd probably said as much as her mother could handle for one day.

Chapter 31

# Sleigh Bells Ring

It was well past noon on Christmas Day when the group settled into the parlor to hear the Christmas story and open gifts. Brianna sat in the middle of the couch and pulled her mother and Tiny down beside her. Fab took the wing chair opposite Kate.

Christmas lights twinkled on the tree. Outside the window, snow hung heavy on the bare branches of the trees. Helena went to the window for a better view. Surveying the snow, she breathed, "Monet might have painted this scene."

Kate sat with a giant Bible on her lap. "The snow *is* pretty."

She adjusted her glasses. "Helena, Fabian, we are so glad you can be with us today. We want to spend a few moments remembering that we're celebrating the birth of our Lord Jesus. Please listen as I read the Christmas story from Luke 2.

*"So Joseph also went up from the town of Nazareth in Galilee to Judea, to Bethlehem the town of David, because he belonged to the house and line of David. He went there to register with Mary, who was pledged to be married to him and was expecting a child. While they were there, the time came for the baby to be born, and she gave birth to her firstborn, a son. She wrapped him in cloths and placed him in a manger, because there was no guest room available for them.*

*And there were shepherds living out in the fields nearby, keeping watch over their flocks at night. An an-*

She closed the book and looked up. "Imagine! When our Savior was born, the angels celebrated and the heavens showed off the glory of God. Today, the snow that fell from heaven covers the dingy side yard and the remains of the garden. 'Tis a reminder that our Savior came to cover our sins and failures."

Everyone turned toward the window. As they looked, some snow piled on the window ledge fell to the ground with a soft "puff" sound. Brianna had never felt such peace. Her heart was lifted by a deep awareness of God's presence. Did her mother and uncle sense it too?

She hated to break the spell, but it was time to open gifts, so she made a quick trip upstairs to retrieve presents for her mother and Fab. When she returned, Kate clapped her hands to silence the chatter in the room.

Brianna handed out the few Christmas presents, and then Tiny eagerly gave her a gift with lovely wrapping.

"Open this first," he said. "June wrapped it for me yesterday at the Co-op."

"Tell June thanks," Brianna said as she lifted out a framed picture. "Oh! I forgot Mona and Craig took photos that night. Thank you!"

She turned the frame around to show off the picture they had posed for at the Fireman's Ball. The camera had captured them looking at each other with delight and amusement. He was handsome in his new suit and new confidence, and her white stole fell away from her shoulders to reveal the silky red dress underneath.

It was quiet in the room as they studied the photo.

"That is an incredible picture," Helena finally admitted.

"I asked Mona to enlarge it and frame it for me. She did a great job," Tiny explained.

"Who's Mona?" Helena asked suspiciously.

"She and Craig Hamilton publish the *Cottonwood Times*," Tiny said.

"You know the newspaper publishers?" Helena asked incredulously.

*Maybe she thinks that's like knowing the publisher of the Los Angeles Times,* Brianna thought with a smile.

"Been friends ever since they moved here," Tiny explained.

Brianna studied the photo. "We didn't know this would be our engagement picture."

They shared a private smile before Tiny explained, "I didn't plan to propose that night, but after seeing Bri all dressed up, I couldn't help but ask her to marry me."

Uncle Fab took the photo and studied it closely. "I don't blame you. Our little girl is all grown up."

"It is perfect, but we must hurry." Kate motioned for her guests to continue opening gifts.

"I made a wall hanging for each of you," Brianna said as she handed out the tissue-wrapped gifts.

Tiny read his aloud. "'The steps of a good man are ordered by the Lord. And he delights in his way.' Psalm 37:23." He smiled appreciatively.

"And the greatest of these is love," Kate read. "I'm honored, Brianna. The sunflowers will even match the yellow in my bedroom."

Uncle Fab and Helena each received a "Faith, Hope & Love" wall hanging. The saying was Brianna's most popular work.

"How can I thank you?" Fab asked as he clutched the plaque to his chest, but Helena said coolly, "So these are the signs you're selling? I don't think they'll catch on."

No one uttered a word for several seconds. Tiny slipped his hand into Brianna's. Finally, she found her voice and responded. "They have already caught on. The orders keep coming in. A chain of arts and crafts stores has offered a contract for supplying them."

There were encouraging murmurs around the room.

Helena shrugged her shoulders. "Maybe I'm wrong."

Finally, Helena and Fab opened their plastic grocery bags from Tiny. "Sorry, I didn't wrap them better," he apologized. "It was kind of last minute."

The bags each held a warm hat, scarf and mittens.

"Good job, Tiny," Kate nodded to Tiny. Then she explained, "I called him early this morning to see if he had a way to secure warm clothing for you."

"It was easy. The sales rep was in last week and filled up the mitten rack at the Co-op. I just went in and picked out what I thought might work."

"That's what I mean," Brianna said to her mother. "Tiny has connections."

Kate beamed and clapped her hands again. "You'll need those warm items. My gift to all of you is a ride in a horse-drawn sleigh."

"Listen, I think they're here!" Tiny said. Everyone quit talking and the sound of bells jingling grew louder. They hurried to the window. A team of chestnut horses and a black sleigh stopped on the snowy street. The horses snorted and shook their heads as steam puffed from their nostrils.

"You're giving us rides in a real sleigh?" Helena asked.

Kate came up behind them. "Yes. That's Ed Carson. He rents quite a bit of my land and we've been friends for years. I called him this morning and asked if by chance he was hitching up his team today. He was, and he volunteered to give rides."

Tiny and Uncle Fab hustled into coats, caps and mittens, while Brianna wrapped Helena and her silky outfit in Kate's long winter coat. When they were ready to leave, Kate waved them off saying she needed a nap more than she needed to go dashing through the snow.

Mr. Carson stood beside the sleigh wearing a heavy coat and a plaid cap with earflaps. The antique sleigh had a seat for the driver and one in the back for passengers. Brianna climbed in next to Helena, expecting Tiny to sit next to her. Instead, Uncle Fab squeezed in the back seat. Tiny shrugged and climbed up to share the driver's seat.

Ed Carson covered the passengers with a furry blanket, and then swung up to his seat. He shook the reins and clucked his tongue. The horses snorted and the sleigh lurched forward for a trip along Main Street. The gliding sensation of riding over the snowy street thrilled Brianna, but soon they turned off the road and bumped through a ditch and into open prairie.

The whiteness of the land was so bright, even Helena had to squint. "It's like being in the movie *Dr. Zhivago*," she cried, and Brianna knew Kate had scored a hit with her mother.

The sound of the runners on the snow, the jingle of the horse tack and the clomp of horse hooves seemed like a prairie concert to Brianna. By the time they got back to the house, the cold had seeped beneath her earmuffs, and all of their faces were snow-flecked and stiff from cold.

Once inside, they stomped the snow from their boots, all trying at once to tell Kate about their exciting trip and thanking her for the gift. Apple cider scented the house and invited them to warm up with the hot spicy drink. Brianna ladled cups of cider and topped them with a frothy batter and nutmeg. Then she pulled the meat, cheese and veggie trays from the fridge and shook crackers into baskets. Helena opened up the platters of cookies, candy and nuts.

Instead of going into the dining room, they sat around the kitchen table and talked about the sleigh ride. That led to stories of other adventures and a lot of laughter. Her mother was mostly civil and Uncle Fab hadn't mentioned his mini bar, although he did smell strangely of peppermint. Brianna wondered if he'd carried a spare bottle of schnapps in his suitcase.

Brianna squeezed Tiny's hand under the table as she listened quietly to the banter in the room. The pale sun was sinking into the western horizon outside the frost-lined kitchen window, and twilight painted soft rainbow colors across the sky.

This is how a family Christmas should be. Perhaps here, in this cozy kitchen, the ice in her mother's heart would melt. Perhaps the tension and disapproval she'd felt all of her life would fade away.

# Chapter 32

# Tiny's True Character

As they lounged around Kate's place early Christmas night, Tiny received a call asking for help with a flat tire. It offered the perfect excuse for Tiny and Brianna to slip away for a while as Kate, Helena and Uncle Fab discussed whether to play *Yahtzee* or *Trivial Pursuit*. Brianna noted that her mother now wore a heavy cardigan over her silk outfit.

Tiny waited while Brianna backed her truck out of the garage. Parking inside was one benefit of Marge and Wayne being away on vacation. When they came back, Brianna would need to park on the street. She didn't look forward to mornings when she needed to let the truck warm up while she scraped frost from the windows.

Tiny whistled when he saw the vibrant blue truck under the streetlight for the first time since it was painted. He walked around the vehicle, and then climbed into the passenger seat. "Wow, they even jazzed up the inside," he said as he ran his hand over the dashboard.

"I couldn't be happier with it." She backed onto the street and drove toward the stop sign on the edge of town. She loved the feel of the truck's steering wheel in her hands and the solid way it held to the road. After the busy and sometimes tense day, going for a drive with Tiny was exactly what she needed to begin to relax.

Cole Jensen waited in his car at the Co-op until they pulled up. Tiny had met the college freshman through the youth group. Cole's parents had abandoned him and he'd been raised by his great-grandmother, Sadie Jensen.

When she went into the nursing home, Amber and Kelly had invited him to live with them when he wasn't in school. Sadly, Sadie had died recently.

"Sorry to ruin your Christmas," Cole said to Tiny. He nodded shyly to Brianna. "I pulled the midnight shift at the convenience store in Minot or I wouldn't have called."

"No problem. It felt good to get out," Tiny said cheerfully as he checked the spare tire on one wheel and the flat tire in the trunk. Squatting down he checked the treads on the other tires.

"How was Christmas at the Jorgensen's?" he asked as he stood up and wiped off his hands with a blue hanky from his back pocket.

Cole grinned. "A lot of fun! Amber's brothers are crazy and the food was boss. I've never had a Christmas like that before."

"Gotta agree they know how to have a good time." Tiny put his gloves back on. "Your front tires are in good shape. We could repair that flat, but you know what? I think a couple new back tires are in order."

"I wish I could afford that, but I better stick with the patch. Money's a little tight."

"The tires will be a gift from me," Tiny clarified.

"Oh no, I can't let you do that."

"I can't let you do that either," Brianna said to Tiny. "I insist on paying for half."

"She's had an eventful day," Tiny noted to Cole. "I wouldn't argue with her." He opened the big door to the garage and Cole drove in. Thirty minutes later, he drove off with two new tires. As they watched his taillights disappear, Brianna hugged Tiny.

"You shouldn't have done that," they said at the same time, then laughed.

"Can you afford to spend that kind of money?" Tiny asked.

"I just got a nice check for my last project," she explained. "And I'm not paying rent. How about you? How can you swing big gifts when you're starting a new business?"

Tiny shrugged. "I don't pay rent, either, and I've learned that when I give, God gives back to me. There's even a scripture about God opening the windows of heaven."

"You must have a special place in God's heart, as well as mine."

"You're pretty open-handed yourself. So when do I get to see my gift?" he asked.

"You want to see the Johnson place now? It's dark and there isn't any electricity in it."

"I have the key and plenty of flashlights," Tiny said, holding up the metal object.

A few minutes later, they unlocked the door to the old car dealership, garage and filling station. Walking carefully, they beamed their flashlights along the walls and floor as they strolled through the large showroom and a suite of offices. The garage took up the whole west side of the building.

When they emerged, Brianna voiced her concern. "Maybe this is a mistake. Remodeling is going to take a lot of work and we don't know for sure what we'll do with the building."

"I think if the deal goes through, we're going to have so many ideas for this space that we'll have to toss a bunch of them out," Tiny declared.

"Name a few."

"We could move my gym in there or finish off a studio for you or open a teen center or rent out some of the space. We could even make an apartment and live there or rent it out."

Brianna climbed back into her truck. Each of those ideas had crossed her mind, but the building would need a lot of updating. Was fixing it up an impossible dream?

They decided to cruise around Cottonwood City and check out the Christmas lights. People went all out with their yard displays so the whole town was cheery and bright. *The Cottonwood Times* offered the incentive of prizes for the homes with the best decorations.

Back in Schulteville, a party was in full swing. Kate and Helena were so focused on a game of *Yahtzee* that they didn't notice their arrival. A Bing Crosby Christmas CD blared and a dish of chocolate covered cherries was empty.

Uncle Fab bopped through the kitchen door with a glass in his hand. His eyes got big when he saw Brianna and Tiny. "Oops!" he said and disappeared back into the kitchen again.

Brianna and Tiny exchanged looks, and then she took off after her uncle. He was lugging his mini bar back into the pantry when she opened the door. "Uncle Fab!"

"What?" he asked innocently. In one smooth action, he set down his treasure, closed the pantry door and leaned against it. Brianna could smell alcohol clear across the room.

"What's up?" Tiny asked as he came into the kitchen.

"Uncle Fab said he wouldn't drink while he was here. Now he's broken his promise."

Tiny surveyed the room. A half-full glass sat on the table and the top of an empty bottle stuck out of the wastebasket. Uncle Fab wore a smirk on his flushed face.

Tiny Winger was an easygoing man. Mellow. Tolerant. However, in this moment, he was mostly a product of his life experiences. A graduate of the school of hard knocks. The butt of jokes because of his size and troubled family. Abused by his alcoholic father. Neglected by his mentally ill mother.

Tiny stood almost a head taller than Brianna's uncle did. His velvet blue eyes had turned the color of stormy water. When he stepped forward, Fab's smirk disappeared.

*Tiny is so strong, he could send Uncle Fab into the next county,* Brianna thought. Then the kitchen door swung open and Kate and Helena appeared.

"What is going on?" Kate asked.

Tiny never took his eyes off Fab, who seemed to shrink as Tiny loomed over him. "Aunt Kate, this guy owes you an apology for drinking in your house. He's got a snoot full."

"Fab means no harm. He can't help himself," Helena cooed.

Kate fanned herself vigorously. "Drinking in my house? Lord deliver us from evil."

Tiny stayed focused on Uncle Fab. "I thought you were some refined person. Yet, you don't have any manners and you've insulted your hostess by breaking her rules. Why?"

"A little drink or two doesn't make a difference." Fab gave his most angelic look.

"What happens if you can't have a drink?" Tiny pressed in. "What's the longest you can go without hitting the sauce? Ever feel sick or get the shakes?"

Brianna frowned. She had always thought Uncle Fab was a social drinker like her parents. What was Tiny seeing in Fab?

Helena clucked her tongue and glared at him. "Don't accuse my brother of being an alcoholic."

Tiny turned to Helena and said softly, "I didn't accuse him of being an alcoholic. But, maybe you should ask yourself if the shoe fits. Does he drink alone? Lie about his drinking? Is his life affected by booze? Has he had any trouble keeping a job?"

*Bullseye,* Brianna thought.

Tiny's shoulders relaxed. "Hey, it's not shameful to be an alcoholic. It's a disease. But, there is something shameful about not helping somebody who's sick." Then his voice softened, but his words seemed to suck the air out of the room. "I know a lot about this because alcohol killed my dad."

He turned to leave and then looked back at Fab. "You owe Miss Schulte an apology."

Brianna followed close behind Tiny, grabbing her coat as they strode out into the icy air. Her mind whirled. Her fiancé had just thrown a landmine into the middle of her family.

"I'm sorry. I don't know what got into me. Now they'll really hate me. Not to mention I made a fool out of myself and ruined Christmas."

Brianna shook her head. "Don't apologize. Everything you said is true. You saw what was going on and stood up for Kate. I'm proud of you. Your noble character is showing through.  And Tiny?"

"What?"

She wrapped her arms around him. "We're in this together."

# Chapter 33

# *The Spider*

Brianna was relieved to find that Helena and Uncle Fab had hurried upstairs for the night. Kate was sitting in the kitchen lost in thought when Brianna sank into a chair next to her.

"We had such good intentions for today," she moaned. "How could it end so badly?"

Kate patted her hand. "It didn't go as we hoped, but God is more interested in building our character than in our comfort. Tonight Tiny pierced your mother and uncle's hearts with the truth. I'm so proud of that boy. I hope he doesn't feel guilty for speaking out."

"I also had an unsettling talk with Helena," Brianna said. "I told her about my faith in God and she told me they planned to kidnap me and take me back with them."

"So they did have ulterior motives for coming here. I'm not surprised that this wasn't just a friendly visit."

"Did Fab apologize before they went upstairs? Did Helena?" Brianna asked.

"Not really. Fabian was quiet. Helena took him upstairs to rest. She put her arm around him and led him out like a child who had just been mistreated."

"It feels like a bomb has hit my family."

Kate smiled. "Now, don't be discouraged. If we had watched football today, we might have seen a good life lesson. Never call the game at half-time."

Brianna sighed and laid her head on Kate's shoulder as the older woman continued. "Your family is unhappy because you're rocking their boat. You've rejected their lifestyle and you're telling them about your new faith. How they respond is not your responsibility."

"It's hard. I feel torn between wanting their approval and living my own life. I guess whatever happens next won't surprise me."

She said goodnight, went up to her room, and opened her Bible to Isaiah 61. The words flowed through her spirit like soothing silk, bringing promises that encouraged. "For those who grieve," she read, "he gives beauty for ashes and the oil of joy for mourning."

Dwelling on the hopeful, comforting words, she almost didn't notice when a note was slipped under her door. Retrieving it, she opened it to her mother's handwriting. "Come to my room for a bit. We can sit by the fireplace and talk."

Brianna bookmarked the page where she was reading. Kate had given her an early Christmas gift of parfait pink flannel pajamas and a robe. She changed into them, closed the door to her room and walked down the hall.

Soon mother and daughter were sitting before the holly-sprigged mantel as warmth radiated from the fireplace. It was the first time the new fireplace had been put to use. She was happy that she'd opted for an electric insert. It was much easier to plug it in than to build a wood fire. Plus, trying to restore the chimney would have taken months.

Helena launched into her topic right away. "Your young man was out of line tonight and your uncle and I are very troubled about what he said. I'm even more troubled to think you would consider marrying someone like that."

"Like what? Someone who calls a spade a spade?"

"You know what I mean. He was insulting tonight. He's simple and uneducated. And, good grief, he must be thirty pounds overweight. What do you see in him?"

Brianna said as she stared into the flames, "I see the future. A future here where I'm free to live my own life. I see a man who adores me and whom I trust and love. Helena, do you love Daddy?"

"There you go again, switching the subject. Stop this nonsense. I want you to pack up and come back with us."

Brianna looked up at the top of the wall. This fall she and Amber had painted this room and it looked so clean. They'd worked hard but had an equal amount of fun. However, she wouldn't open that fond memory to her mother's ridicule.

"Brianna, you must listen to me. Don't do anything rash, like get married. This is a passing phase. You'll get tired of the bitter cold and you were made for greater things than remodeling old houses or slapping paint on wooden boards. Sooner or later, you need to come home and take your rightful place."

Brianna felt like a knife blade had pierced her heart. She was already tired of the cold. Would she get tired of Cottonwood, too? Was this a temporary escape for her? Was Tiny an infatuation? The bed and breakfast, Davis Designs, her romance with Tiny had all happened fast. Maybe too fast.

Helena must have seen her pause, because she continued to plead her case. "When you were quite young, Princess Diana and Prince Charles were married. It was the wedding of the century. That's when I decided that I'd give you a wonderful wedding. I envisioned you in silk and lace. Flowers everywhere. The finest food and wine and music."

Helena's vision of a wedding was strikingly like her own long-held dreams. Her uncertainty must have registered on her face.

Helena recognized her advantage. "Here's what I want you to do. Put off marrying for at least a year. If you're truly in love, a year won't matter. Don't rush into marriage with—what is his real name anyway?"

Brianna watched a black spider make its way out of

the molding near the ceiling and drop down the wall. Were spiders invading this freshly redecorated space?

Leaping up, she grabbed a magazine and whapped the spider, which dropped to the floor.

Helena jumped.

"Spider," Brianna explained. Thoughts flooded her mind. She decided not to sit down again but to wade into this battle standing on her feet.

"Will Daddy be around to give me away next year?" she asked as she disposed of the unfortunate spider.

"I'm sure we can work that out."

"Must the wedding be in California?"

"Yes! There are so many beautiful venues there. Besides, planning will be much easier if the wedding is nearby."

"But it isn't your wedding, it's ours," Brianna cried. "I'll admit I remember Diana's wedding and always wanted a beautiful wedding dress and the works. However, nothing in me wants to have the wedding there. This is my home now. Tiny and I want to get married here among *our* friends."

"If you want us to pay for this wedding, then you must do it my way."

"Your way? Sounds like this is your wedding. What about Daddy? Isn't he the one who foots the bills?"

"Yes, but he'll agree."

"Helena, I have an idea. Maybe instead of planning *my* wedding, you should live on the same continent as Daddy. You could plan a fancy anniversary party for yourselves and renew your vows. Tiny and I are quite able to pay for our own wedding."

Brianna moved toward the door. Everything she'd said was true, but she was disappointed in herself for the sarcastic tone in her voice. She hated to leave on that note, but she was afraid of what else she might say.

"Brianna, don't go away angry!" Helena called after her.

At the door, she bowed her head and took a deep breath. Tears filled her eyes. Finally, she turned to face her mother.

"I've always wanted your approval, but nothing I do is good enough for you. I welcomed you into my new life and tried to overlook your contempt for my new faith and the man I want to marry. I'm through trying to win your approval."

Brianna slipped out the door and stood in the hallway for a moment. She could hear the steady tick of the grandfather clock on the landing. How many years had it stood there, steadily keeping the minutes, hours and days? Then she heard a rustling sound coming from her room.

Slowly opening the door, she caught a whiff of musky shaving lotion. Quickly opening the door, she flipped on the light. No one was there, but she noted the door between her room and the Jack and Jill bath was ajar. Looking beyond the door, she saw Fab swaying in the doorway to his bedroom.

Brianna slammed the door shut and fled downstairs. Her thoughts ping-ponged around in her head. Mindful that Kate was asleep in the next room, instead of pacing the parlor, she reached behind the sofa for the soft yellow afghan that was used for napping. Wrapping it around her, Brianna snuggled into the sofa.

The connection between her nightmares and her uncle's musky presence was odd. She fingered the edge of her pajamas as she worked through her fright. She had always suppressed her negative feelings about Uncle Fab. Since he was her mother's charming brother, she had always thought her feelings were unjustified.

Now she wondered if he was the man of her nightmares.

# Chapter 34

# The Eye of the Storm

From the depths of her coma-like sleep, Brianna heard the clock toll twice. She opened one eye. Kate stood over her wearing an enormous white flannel nightgown.

"Huh!" Brianna jerked upright. "You look like a ghost!"

"Hush. Why are you sleeping here?" Kate whispered.

Brianna fell back on the couch. *Why am I sleeping here, anyway? Oh. Uncle Fab's visit.*

"Come with me," Kate urged. Once they were settled in the privacy of Kate's bedroom, Brianna realized she didn't know where to begin explaining what happened. How Helena had almost persuaded her to go back to California. Her final words to Helena. The smell in her room that sent her fleeing downstairs. The memories that forced their way to the surface of her mind.

"It's the middle of the night. Maybe we should talk in the morning," she hedged.

"We'll talk right now," Kate whispered in her school superintendent's voice.

"I had a conversation with my mother and it didn't end well. When I went back to my room, I could smell musky aftershave in there. It was for real this time. I peeked in the bathroom and there was Uncle Fab watching me. It creeped me out. The door to the bathroom was open. I know I closed it."

"So you think Fabian was in your room." It was a statement.

"It was like a lightbulb went on in my head and I remembered some things. The smell of that shaving lotion took me back to when I was growing up. All of the parties we had at our house. All of the leers and suggestive comments made to me."

"Brianna, I'm going to ask you the big question. Do you remember being molested at any of those parties?"

"No. I don't think that ever happened, but one person made me uncomfortable. It never led to anything, but sometimes he wanted me to sit on his lap or he'd tickle me. I tried to avoid being alone with him. I associate the shaving lotion with those icky feelings."

"Fabian."

"Yes. Uncle Fab. It only happened when he'd been drinking a lot. He was always at our house because he was Helena's 'darling' brother and her pet project. Helena always helped Fab when he lost a job or had some other bad luck. She covered for him. She gave him money and supplied him with booze."

"So Tiny was correct about Fabian having a problem. Did Fabian go along to England when your parents moved there?"

"No. He went to visit them, but to be honest, I don't think Daddy likes him very well, either. He came back to the States a few months before Helena."

Brianna stopped and put her head in her hands. She must have subconsciously known much of what she'd just told Kate. However, tonight was the first time she'd put so many pieces of her life together. "I'm only now grasping all of this."

"Someone said that knowledge is power." Kate patted her hand. "And our Lord Jesus said, 'You shall know the truth, and the truth shall set you free.' Brianna, I believe you and Tiny broke open a mystery that will bring about healing for you and your family."

Brianna looked into Kate's steady gray eyes. If wisdom and kindness had colors, she knew they would have the same hue as those eyes.

When Brianna awoke the next morning, the sun was shining and Kate was gone. Voices were murmuring in the dining room. She stretched lazily. For a few moments, she entertained the idea of staying in bed all day to avoid facing Helena and Uncle Fab.

Then Kate opened the door.

"I'm glad you're awake." Kate eased onto a straight-backed chair near the bed. "Your mother looks like she hasn't slept all night. She was on the phone for an hour trying to book plane reservations for today."

Brianna groaned. Tranquility was so fleeting.

"Imagine demanding reservations on the day after Christmas," Kate opined. "It's a wonder she could get anything this week, but they're flying out tomorrow morning."

"It's just as well that they leave. I really don't want to see either of them unless they can deal with their issues. And I'm worried about how Tiny is coping."

"Tiny is a big boy. He can take care of himself."

"Maybe, but I want to make his life better rather than worse."

"This has been difficult and there are things you'll need to work through, but try to put this day in God's hands and see what happens."

Brianna sighed. How nice it would be to put her hair in a ponytail, step into her work clothes and lose herself in an art project. Or tear the wallpaper off Uncle Fab's bedroom.

Instead, she went up to the bathroom, locked the doors, and took a hot shower. She felt like she was putting on war paint when she put on her makeup. Her blue suede boots, skinny jeans and a warm white tunic felt like a suit of armor.

When her cellphone rang, she was relieved to hear Amber's voice.

"I'm calling to invite you over for an impromptu lunch."

"We have company," Brianna answered, her voice flat. "My mother and Uncle Fab showed up on Christmas Eve and they're leaving tomorrow."

"I heard about your Christmas, including the meltdown between Tiny and your mother and uncle."

Brianna looked at the clock. It wasn't even midmorning. News traveled around Cottonwood Creek faster than a sports car on a speedway.

"Kelly stopped at the Co-op early this morning. I think Tiny needed to talk."

She was relieved that Tiny was able to talk to Kelly, who was as wise as an owl. She desperately needed a girlfriend talk right now.

"It was like a television Christmas comedy or maybe a tragedy. I don't think you really want us to come over for lunch. Everything is too raw."

"Yes, we do want you to come. You know how good Kelly is at calming situations. Just tell your family that Kelly would love to see them and I want to meet them before they leave."

Brianna doubted Kelly would *love* to see her mother, although the idea of stopping by the parsonage strongly appealed to her.

"Really, I've made a lovely turkey and vegetable soup that is so healthy and low calorie that even your mother will appreciate it. I plan to make Monte Cristo sandwiches with the leftover ham. Of course, we have desserts, that's plural. It turns out that Adam's fiancé, Lorie, loves to bake, too. We have pies we haven't even sliced."

"Alright. I'll run it by Helena and Uncle Fab. Would one o'clock work?"

"You betcha. As soon as I hear back from you, I'll put Mildred in the garage."

Brianna smiled and nodded. The less she saw of their cat, the better. But, the thought that her good friends were once again standing with her was uplifting. When she entered the dining room a couple minutes later, she heard voices in the kitchen. She stopped behind the partially open door and listened. Apparently, their conversation had been going on for a long time.

"You must have been close to your brother, too." Helena was speaking.

"Ted was the most Christ-like person I've ever known. After being away at college for a few years, Ted came back to be pastor of Cross Church. I moved home a few years later when I was asked to be superintendent of schools. Neither of us married. We just lived here where we were born and took care of our parents."

Brianna peeked around the door. The two women were seated at the table. Helena hadn't combed her hair and her face was puffy and blotched, like she had cried all night. Even more shocking, she was eating a piece of cherry kuchen.

"I'm sure you are as devoted to Fabian as I was to Ted. We sisters can be mother hens."

Helena nodded. "Our parents died young and mother begged me to watch after Fab when she knew she wouldn't make it. They left us some money, but otherwise we were on our own. We were far from ready to take care of ourselves. Fab made some poor choices and squandered his inheritance."

"So you rescued him."

"I thought I was doing the right thing."

"Doing the right thing depends on a lot of factors. Is Fabian mentally or physically challenged? Then of course you must care for him."

"Oh, there's nothing wrong with him, except he can't make it on his own."

"Why not?"

"I. Well. He."

"Perhaps it's time to consider giving him the space and dignity to stand on his own."

"Put that way..."

"I supervised thousands of children going through school and I learned that when we give young people confidence in themselves, they often find a way to lead successful lives. Last spring many former students came back for the closing of Cross Church. There were leaders in government, education and business. Oh, it did my heart good to see them."

"I can imagine."

"You haven't warmed up to Tiny yet, but you have my word that he is a success story in the making. And Kelly. To think what he went through with his brother's death. Yet he overcame his grief. I believe Kelly is of the same spirit as my brother Ted. As I said earlier, I'm as proud of Tiny, Kelly and Brianna as if they were my own."

"Brianna is my very own, but somehow I lost her." Tears trickled from Helena's eyes.

Chapter 35

# The Blue Angel

The conversation paused between Kate and her mother, and Brianna stepped hesitantly into the room.

"Darling." Her mother rose from her chair and held out her arms. Brianna stood bewildered for a moment. Was Helena changing or was this another ploy? Kate's nod pushed her toward her mother's hug. With her mother's arms wrapped around her, all of the emotions she had held back for years played across her heart.

"Helena, I'm sorry I was cross last night," she whispered.

"You have no reason to be sorry." Helena's voice sounded strangled, as if a wad of jelly filled her throat. "I was up most of the night thinking and you were right about so much. I was only seeing your life from my point of view. I don't want to lose you."

Briana couldn't say anything as tears sheeted down her face. Finally, after Kate coughed politely, she backed away. They wiped their tears away with the backs of their hands and hiccupped at the same time.

"It might not be easy, but I promise I'll try to let you make your own decisions."

Brianna wasn't gullible. They had a lot of damage to repair in their relationship and it would take work. Still, maybe her mother was beginning to thaw.

"I hear you're leaving tomorrow."

"Yes. I need to take Fab home and I have some thinking to do."

"Where is Fab?" Brianna dreaded seeing him. At some point, she needed to tell Helena about Fab's folly. Would Helena believe her or would she dismiss her words and take Fab's side? She needed to tell Tiny, too, but for now it seemed best to let things cool down.

"Fabian polished off some cinnamon toast," Kate said. "Then went back to his room."

Brianna sighed in relief.

"Would you like to get out of the house with me today?" she asked Helena. "Amber invited us for lunch. You could see Kelly and meet Amber. We can drive through Cottonwood City on the way. What do you say?"

Helena hesitated at first, fingering her hair before agreeing to go. An hour later, Brianna knocked on her bedroom door and urged her to hurry. Her mother didn't go out in public unless she looked like a well-preserved debutante, not an easy task if she'd cried all night.

When Helena finally appeared, she showed no sign of droopy hair or puffy eyes. Walking down the steps with the grace of a princess, her elegance belied the fact that she wore a pair of borrowed long johns and a warm shirt under her dressy pantsuit to ward off the winter chill.

"I guess it's just you and me," Brianna said. Helena had checked with Fab, but he was still under the weather, and Kate had a meeting. Tiny couldn't get away because the Co-op was extra busy. She promised to stop by for a moment when they were in town.

Brianna had let the truck idle in front of the house so that it was warm as cocoa. She thought the vibrant blue paint was quite striking against the white snow.

"What is that?" Helena asked when they walked out the door. "Where's your car?"

"These are my wheels now. It was a milk delivery truck. Isn't it cool? I had it tuned up, painted and restored. It came back from the shop just before you arrived."

"You can't be serious about driving around in this, this, antique lorry."

Brianna studied the paint job. There were angel's wings painted into the design. "Huh. Angel wings. I think I'll name her the Blue Angel," she said as she opened the passenger door for her mother. A wave of warm air met them. Helena climbed in, her lips pursed in disapproval. Brianna smiled sweetly, but slammed the door shut as hard as she could.

When they arrived in Cottonwood City, she drove up Main Street, pointing out the beauty shop, hardware store and bank where she did business. Then she pulled in by Amber's insurance office. "I wish I could take you inside to see how nice we made Amber's office, but at least you can picture where it is if I mention it."

She pulled away, driving slowly past the Johnson gas station. How she wanted to announce she was buying it, but instead, she pointed it out as a town landmark. "I've heard there are very few buildings with that iconic design."

Helena leaned forward and stared at the building. "Someone should tear it down and put it out of its misery."

Brianna sighed and put on the turn signals to go around the block. She pulled in by Tiny's Gym where they could see a couple people inside using the equipment. "Tiny just opened this and he already has dozens of memberships. Amber and I did the decorating for this, too."

Helena peered through the window. "There are hardly any machines."

"True, but he'll add more in time. This is a small town and people are glad to have a place to exercise." She tried to keep the frustration out of her voice.

She could only tolerate so much scorn, so she elected to tour a stately neighborhood of two-story homes rather than drive past the mobile home Tiny shared with his mother.

Finally, she drove by the auditorium where the Fireman's Ball was held. "This is where Tiny proposed, right over there in that little garden." The memory made her feel gooey inside.

"How romantic," her mother replied dryly.

*So much for being more accepting*, Brianna thought. She was ready to make her own sarcastic remark when she looked at the ceiling of the truck, hoping to see a spider she could swat. Instead, she noticed a sticker just above her head. It read, "With God all things are possible." *Who put that there?* she wondered.

Before leaving town, she pulled into the Co-op and beeped the horn. Tiny appeared wearing his green Co-op cap and greasy coveralls. She cranked down the window.

"Hey, it's the Mango Queen and her blue machine," he quipped as he put his elbows on the window. Then he looked past Brianna. "Hello, Mrs. Davis." Helena gave him a faint smile.

Brianna gave him her flirty smile. "A Christmas elf put a sticker on the ceiling. Do you know anything about that?"

"Depends. Do you like the sticker?"

"I do. Every time I look up, I'll be reminded of God's faithfulness."

"Then let's just say a mighty big elf put it there." They smiled at each other for a long moment that might have become a kiss if her mother hadn't been present.

"I took Helena on a tour of the town on our way to lunch. Sorry you can't join us today."

"Me, too, but the cold weather causes a lot of problems with batteries and other car parts. June is even staying all afternoon to help in the store.

"Amber's a real good cook, Mrs. Davis. I'm sure you'll have a fine time." He slapped the top of the truck in farewell and went back inside.

Brianna again toyed with the idea of driving by the Winger home. She could tell the funny story about Jolina throwing the cake in her face. No, better to leave Jolina out of this.

Then she looked at Helena. She had expected to be called out for choosing a man who wore coveralls and worked with his hands. Instead, Helena was staring at the note on the ceiling.

"Your father used to leave little notes for me in a dresser drawer or propped against the coffee pot. When did he stop doing that?" *Aha,* Brianna thought, *the ice is beginning to melt.*

"I can imagine Daddy doing that. He writes good letters." They pulled out onto the highway.

"You know, Helena, people here wear a lot of different hats. Tiny is the store clerk, and the manager, bookkeeper, and mechanic at the Co-op. That's what it takes to keep things going in a small town. Amber is the insurance agent and the janitor at her business. Kelly is a pastor, but he also mows the grass."

"That appeals to you?"

"I love the community spirit. That Fireman's Ball that we attended? The firefighters are volunteers who drop everything when the fire whistle blows. The ambulance crew is volunteer, too. There are generations of people here that care for each other. For example, Marge and Wayne moved in with Kate so she can stay in her home. I want that kind of life."

Then, she realized something. "Wow! I just realized why Tiny wants a big wedding. Everyone in town is like part of his family. Of course, he wants to invite them."

Without preface, Helena said, "I always thought you and Kelly would end up together." She sounded wistful, although she hadn't previously been fond of Kelly.

"I wondered about that at one time, too. He looks and talks exactly like Kyle. However, when we finally got around to sharing a kiss it was clear that he wasn't Kyle. We're meant to only be friends."

"Too bad," Helena commented and then retreated into her own thoughts. Meanwhile, Brianna fled into a world of silent prayer as they rolled down the narrow highway in the Blue Angel.

Chapter 36

# *The Turkey Bone Soup Debacle*

Brianna and Helena rode in silence on the way to lunch. As the truck topped a hill, the steeple of Cottonwood Church appeared in elegant relief against the azure sky. Next, the church appeared, blending into the snow-covered prairie like a rabbit with a white winter coat. The frozen creek bed, footbridge, and a trio of deer completed the picture.

"Isn't it beautiful? Like sparkly light from heaven." She pulled to the side of the road to drink in the view. *This is where I want to be married, in this church, with all of our friends sharing the day.*

Breaking out of her reverie, she explained. "Kelly and Amber live on the other side of these trees." She pointed out the gazebo, which seemed to float on top of the snow. "That's where they were married. Where I first saw Tiny. And where I broke my ankle." *A lot of memories were made in that one spot.* "We're early for lunch. Let's stop at the church for a moment."

*What will Helena think of this place?* They pulled up next to the building and walked up the short sidewalk past a simple manger scene. Inside, their footsteps echoed across the wooden vestibule floor. They stopped at the door of the sanctuary and peeked inside.

Light flowed through the windows and danced over every surface. The window ledges held fragrant greenery and white candles, while the pews were decorated with red bows. Behind the altar, an evergreen forest parted in honor of the cross that hung on the wall.

Helena's eyes swept the country church. "There is an unusual ambiance here."

Brianna nodded eagerly, thankful that her mother could tell there was something different about the church, even if she didn't know how to express it.

"I've been here every Sunday through the Christmas season, but didn't notice how beautifully Amber had decorated."

"When it's filled with people you probably see them instead," Helena answered perceptively.

*True,* Brianna thought. The reserved, steadfast people that filled the sanctuary each Sunday intrigued her. The gray heads and straight shoulders of long-time members. The energy of the young people who claimed the pews on the east side closest to the front. Families, like the McLeans, who filled whole rows.

She took a step toward the front of the church, and then another. "This would be a perfect time for a wedding," Brianna blurted. Proceeding slowly up the center aisle, she could imagine Tiny waiting for her at the front, could almost hear the joyful music.

"Perhaps you should snap a few photos so the décor can be copied."

"Copied?"

"Yes, so if you have your wedding here next Christmas, you can remember how it looks."

"Ah, yes. I'll try to do that," Brianna responded. "Right now, we better hurry over to Kelly and Amber's. We don't want to be late."

Thoughts raced through her mind on the short trip to the parsonage next door. She wasn't about to tell her mother that she hoped to hold the wedding very soon. First, she must ask Kelly if it was even possible. Then she needed to ask Tiny if he was ready to take the big step. No use in opening the topic with her mother yet.

As they drove into the parsonage yard, Brianna looked at the house and wondered how her mother would view it. A wooden deck was tacked on the east side and a garage attached on the north. A row of barren lilac trees stood to the west. Helena didn't comment.

"This is farm country, so we go in the backdoor to the laundry room and kitchen."

"How peculiar," Helena commented.

"You'll find Amber is informal but very warm. In fact, there she is waving at us through the kitchen window." She waved back and opened her door.

Kelly leaned out of the door to greet them, wearing a flannel shirt and stocking feet. "Welcome! And a belated Merry Christmas," he called out.

Soon Brianna found herself in a bear hug, and when Kelly let go, Amber crushed her in a curly-haired hug.

Kelly's eyes watered as he took both of Helena's hands. "I'm so pleased to see you. We have a lot of catching up to do, but first I want to introduce my wife, Amber Rose McLean Jorgenson." His chest puffed a little in pride.

Amber gave Helena a hug. "It's wonderful to meet Brianna's mom. We've become the dearest friends. But, may I admit I'm nervous? I hear you excel at entertaining."

Helena reacted by self-consciously touching her hair and smiling. Kelly threw their coats on the dryer in the laundry room, as Amber steered Helena into the kitchen.

"I thought Monte Cristo sandwiches would go well with soup on a cold day. Besides, it uses up a lot of leftovers. I'll send some ham home with you for supper, too. Now you must tell me some of your secrets to entertaining. I'm used to cooking for my big family, but I don't know much about formal entertaining."

Amber prattled on as she skillfully layered ham, turkey and Swiss cheese between slices of bread, dipped them in a homemade batter, and browned them in a pan sizzling with butter.

*She butters up my mother as well as she butters that bread*, Brianna thought.

Brianna took the opportunity for a quiet discussion with Kelly in the living room. "We stopped at the church and the Christmas décor inspired me to ask you something. Of course, I need to confirm this with Tiny. No need to bring it up if it's out of the question."

Kelly cocked his head in confusion.

"What I'm trying to ask is whether Tiny and I can get married at the church before the holidays are over."

"Whoa, that's not what I expected to hear. These holidays?" Kelly led her to the far end of the living room out of earshot.

Brianna nodded. "When Helena and I visited the church a few minutes ago, it was like the church was all dressed up with the hope and love of Christmas. I could see myself walking up the aisle."

She lowered her voice to a whisper. "Kelly, now that Helena and Uncle Fab have paid me a visit, I know for certain that I'm ready to stay here at Cottonwood Creek. And I want to spend the rest of my life with Tiny."

"Wow. Having you stay here would be such a blessing. But, are you sure? You shouldn't make a hasty decision just because things didn't go well this week."

"I admit, my relationship with my family needs work, although Daddy wrote to me. Things are better between us. I hope matters will work out with my mother, too. However, getting married now would help avoid more problems. Helena wants to plan a big wedding in California."

She shrugged and smiled. "If that happens, I'll have to find a new groom. Tiny will never let her control our lives.

So, is it possible to hold a simple wedding after the Sunday morning service? And how soon could we do this?”

Kelly smiled. “Tiny would be like a bull in a china closet at one of Helena’s events.”

“Then we can do it?” Brianna gripped Kelly’s arms.

“I’d be more than honored to perform the ceremony. You’ll want at least a week to get your marriage license and contact people. We’ll need to meet a couple times for a prenuptial chat and to plan the ceremony. As for the holiday decorations, we keep them up until after Epiphany in January.”

“I need to talk to Tiny tonight. Thank you so much!” she exclaimed as she threw her arms around Kelly.

Just then, her mother and Amber came through the kitchen door. “Brianna!” Helena said, disapprovingly. She turned to look for Amber’s reaction to the embrace.

“Lunch in two minutes,” Amber called out, clearly unbothered by the hug. She put a platter of sandwiches on the table and returned to the kitchen.

“Helena,” Brianna warned.

Helena shrugged with resignation and then peered closely at the dining and living rooms of the parsonage. A stack of books wobbled on Kelly’s desk. More textbooks were scattered on the floor and Mildred’s bed was tucked near the fireplace.

“This house is...charming.”

“Thank you,” Kelly said affably. “We’re quite comfortable here.”

Then, Helena spied a trophy walleye mounted over the fireplace, and an ‘oh’ escaped from her mouth. “A fish on the wall?”

Brianna cringed. The fish surely offend Helena’s artistic senses. To make matters worse, she knew Tiny had given it to Amber and Kelly as a wedding gift.

Just then, Amber came through the kitchen door and set a kettle of soup on the table. Helena's brow arched for a wrinkle-making moment.

"Soup's on. I hope you like turkey bone soup," Amber said, opening her arms to welcome their guests to take a seat at the dining room table.

After they were seated, Kelly offered up thanks for the food and a blessing on those gathered at the table. Amber served the soup and passed the Monte Cristo sandwiches.

"Whatever is turkey bone soup?" Helena murmured as she eyed the pot in the middle of the table.

"Turkey bone soup is a highly nutritional culinary dish," Brianna declared instantly.

When the sandwiches were passed, Helena refused to take one. "Christmas is over and it's back to careful eating," she explained, pointedly looking at Brianna who had a sandwich halfway to her mouth.

Brianna took a bite and chewed slowly. Did her mother not know she was a San Francisco executive? A woman who had the courage to drive across the country to begin a new life? Who was on her way to becoming a successful entrepreneur? She was certainly able to choose her own diet.

"Amber, these sandwiches are delicious," she said. Her spirit soared like a kite in March wind. The feeling was as delectable as the food. She was free to choose what to eat and how to exercise. She could even decide who to marry, and when and where.

Just as Helena took a sip of soup, Brianna turned to Amber. "If Tiny and I get married next week, will you be my bridesmaid?"

Her mother choked on soup, and then spit carrots and peas across the table.

How Brianna wished she could capture the moment with her camera.

Chapter 37

# Wedding Plans

Brianna delivered Helena to Schulteville late in the afternoon, as the sun dropped below the western horizon. Amber and Kelly had been like balm to a skin rash, calming the situation between mother and daughter, and now Brianna was ready to ask Tiny to marry her.

Helena climbed out of the truck with a shopping bag filled with leftovers, and Brianna sped off through the dusk to Cottonwood City. She hoped it was quiet at the Co-op, so they could have this important talk.

"Important business," she called to June, who was stocking the candy section. Then she whisked Tiny into the back room.

"Hey, hey, what's going on?" Tiny asked as she firmly closed the door behind them.

She wrapped her arms around his neck. "Would you marry me? A week from Sunday?"

"Heck, yes. I'd marry the Mango Queen right now if you gave the word."

"That's good, because I already asked Amber to be my matron of honor. Lots of our friends will already be in church and it's all decorated."

"I like that idea." Tiny stood back. "It lets me off the hook. I was afraid your mom would make me go to California to claim you. But, you wanted to make your own dress and have a fancy wedding. We won't have much time to get ready."

"As crazy as it sounds, I don't care! I see God's blessing in doing it this way."

"Always best to walk the direction He's going," Tiny said wisely. "If He's for us, who can be against us?"

"Yes, and we've had enough against us." She sighed. "And we still have some big things to work out, such as where to live?"

Tiny turned red at the mention of living together. He looked away for a moment and then said, "Don't worry about it, Bri. We have options. My house. Kate's place. Hey, we could even move into Johnson's gas station."

"I actually considered that for about half a second," Brianna said with a smile. "However, that may be more than we can deal with right now. Let's plan to stay at Kate's at first. Now, what about your mother? Do you want her to attend?"

Tiny shook his head. "I'd feel better if we don't tell her until later. What about your mother and uncle?"

"They're leaving in the morning and I don't think they'll be back."

When Brianna arrived home several hours later, she was surprised to see the lights were still on. Kate and Helena sat in the parlor wearing bathrobes and sipping ginger tea, by the scent that wafted through the air. Her mother clutched a wad of tissues in one hand. *Crying again.*

Kate spoke up. "Brianna, dear, take off your wraps and join us. We want to hear what is going on. And I have news for you."

Brianna collapsed onto the couch. How much more news could she handle? She grabbed a frosted snowman cookie off a tray and bit into it. Before trading news stories, there was something she needed to say.

"Helena, I'm sorry about today. I can't live up to your standards anymore and I was afraid you were ready to pass judgment on Kelly and Amber. You know, sometimes, it's okay to serve food from a kettle instead of a tureen and to hang a fish over the fireplace. And I'm finished with being on a diet three hundred and sixty days a year."

Helena buried her face in the tissues. "I'm so sorry. I was way out of line."

"You must have been a terribly shocked when I suddenly asked Amber to be my matron of honor. I regret that, too. You've always had dreams for my wedding and now I'm wrecking them." Then she paused. "Wait. What did you say?"

"Darling, I'm ashamed of my behavior today. You don't need to try to live up to my expectations anymore. Is it too late to start over again?"

The room was silent for a moment except for the ticking of the clock on the landing.

"Of course. You're still my mother. I owe you a lot, but we'll need to make changes in how we treat one another."

"Yes. I want to work on that." The last of Helena's perfect makeup rubbed off as she dried her eyes with the soggy tissues.

Kate interrupted with a polite cough. "I told Helena that God knows all about us and He can be the best friend we've ever had. I encouraged her to talk to Him about her needs and desires. When I think of friends in high places, He is the ultimate."

Helena held up a devotional. "Look, Kate even gave me this book. There's a message in it for each day of the year."

A devotional. Brianna wondered why she hadn't thought of giving her mother a little book of inspiration. Then she took a deep breath. "Okay, on with the news. Tiny and I plan to get married after the morning service a week from Sunday."

Tears popped into her eyes. "I hope you'll both be at the wedding."

"Well, praise the Lord!" Kate fairly shouted. "Helena told me about your big announcement today, but I wondered if you could work it out that quickly."

"We confirmed our plans with Kelly tonight. The ceremony will be at noon. Kelly suggested asking the church ladies to host a reception for us, but I don't know."

"What kind of wedding feast could unprofessional people prepare?" Helena sputtered.

Kate's chin rose. "I must defend the women of the church. They're able to pull together a repast fit for a king. Even out here on the prairie."

Brianna nodded. "Yes, of course they can. Let's do it. I'll ask them to help us. Amber suggested a casual menu of sandwiches and bars."

"Oh!" Helena fanned herself. "It must be something more elegant. If only my favorite caterers could help you! Oysters Rockefeller and sparkling wine for an appetizer. Tai-meshi. Spanakopita. Rack of lamb and carrot soufflé."

"No." Brianna and Kate both scowled at her. "This is exactly the kind of pushiness I won't tolerate anymore."

Helena put her hands to her face. "Oh dear. I can't bear this. A wedding with no bridal showers, rehearsal dinner, banquet, or gift opening. Whatever does Tiny's mother think of all this? She does live here doesn't she?"

Brianna and Kate looked at each other.

"Jolina Winger is not here presently." Kate was a master of telling the truth while giving nothing away.

"Actually, Jolina's in the state mental hospital." Brianna sat perched on the edge of the couch. "She has a form of schizophrenia. We hope treatment will help her lead a normal life." As Brianna spilled the shocking information, relief trickled through her body like rain through a downspout. Secrets were such a heavy burden to bear. She slouched back on the couch.

Helena pursed her lips.

"Mental illness is a disease," Brianna explained. "We shouldn't judge people who have it any more than we'd judge someone who has cancer or diabetes. Or alcoholism," she alluded to Uncle Fab's problem.

Helena looked at her sharply and Kate shook her head. Brianna understood at once that the two women had discussed Fab while she was gone.

"Mrs. Winger's 'disease' must be difficult for Tiny," Helena commented.

"That's a topic for another day," Brianna said sharply. "The wedding was my big news, but, Kate, you haven't shared your news."

"I won't be at your wedding," Kate said.

"What?"

"I made plans this morning to visit a friend in Arizona. He asked me to come down for the month of January. I'll be sitting in the sunshine sipping lemonade on your wedding day. 'Tis a blessing for you, Brianna. If you like, you and Tiny can spend your honeymoon here without me doddering around spying on you."

Brianna swallowed, wondering if she heard right. Did Kate just say she was going to skip her wedding in order to visit a man in Arizona?

"And you, Helena? Will you stay for my wedding?"

Helena looked at the ceiling for a moment. "I don't think so, Darling. We'd just be locked in one battle after another. Besides, I need time to sort all of this out and I want to take Fab home."

It was sad that their parents wouldn't be at their wedding. Yet, it was a sign that they were moving out from under the baggage of their growing up years.

After the women retired to their rooms, Brianna knew she had one more person to tell about the wedding. The thought of it filled her with deep longing. Above all others, she wanted this person's blessing. She picked up her phone to put a call through to London.

When her father answered, she meant to convey her grownup, sophisticated self. But suddenly she felt like she was ten again. "Hello, Daddy? Guess what? I'm getting married!"

Chapter 38

# *The Wedding*

Brianna stood at the back of Cottonwood Church swathed in an off the shoulders cloud of embroidered lace and taffeta.

Everyone at Cottonwood Creek apparently wanted to see Tiny marry the girl from California. The regular attenders scrunched into the middle of the pews as newcomers pushed in from the edges. Rusty and some guys from the bowling team leaned against the back wall. One of the members of the youth group trained a video camera on Brianna, while Mona darted around taking pictures.

Evergreens, white candles and red bows still adorned the church. However, Brianna had added vases of golden silk sunflowers, her personal symbol of new life. Their color popped against the evergreen trees on the stage.

She moved her shoulders, still amazed to be wearing her mother's wedding gown. The man at her side smiled reassuringly and linked arms with her.

Tiny waited for her at the front of the church in the dark suit he'd worn when he proposed. His flaxen hair flowed stylishly over his collar. She was glad there were still hints of the awkward man she'd met at Kelly and Amber's wedding. Even now, his hands were jammed into his pockets and his ears were a charming pink.

Kate had been the one to see the real Tiny when others, including herself, only saw his clumsiness. Kate had called forth a new man. That's what he was now. A new man.

Pastor Kelly and Sheriff Pickle waited on either side of Tiny. *Bill is such a good choice for best man,* she thought, *and a guiding influence for Tiny.* Amber, her matron of honor, sat at the piano watching for Brianna's cue to begin playing.

Brianna touched her dress again. The mailman had made the special delivery the day she and Amber planned to shop for a wedding dress in Bismarck. She'd laid the large box on the dining room table and opened it as Kate and Amber hovered nearby. Yards of white taffeta and lace lay carefully packed beneath an ivory-colored note card.

*Darling Brianna,*

*I'm sending my wedding gown to you. I'd be delighted if you wear it on your wedding day, but whether you do or not, please know I am with you in heart. The inspiration for the dress was the cover of a bridal magazine from the year your father and I married.*

*Love, Mom*

She had stared at the signature. *Mom?* Maybe Helena was changing.

Brianna remembered her mother modeling the dress once, but she hadn't seen it since. She examined the picture and then held up the gown. The dress had an A-line silhouette, cuffed bishop sleeves and a low neckline. French embroidered lace was appliqued to the sleeves, bodice, and skirt. Technically, it was a nineteen seventies prairie dress, but it would be elegant in any era.

"It's perfect. Absolutely perfect!" she had exclaimed. "Look at the details. It must have taken her months to sew it." Brianna had fled upstairs to try on the dress and call her mother. Later, she and Amber drove to Bismarck to purchase a dress for Amber and some smoking hot lingerie for Brianna.

Now, standing at the back of the church, Brianna fingered the sheer white fabric as the man next to her whispered in her ear.

"Honey, you look like your momma in that dress," Eldon Davis told her. "My little Briannie Bee is all grown up and I'm so proud of you."

She hadn't dreamed her father would walk her down the aisle. However, when she called him to say she was getting married, he had moved heaven and earth to take time off. He'd traveled thousands of miles to be here.

He arrived a few days before the wedding, so they had time to talk. She had learned of her father's newfound faith and his thirst to know more. He'd even spent an afternoon plying Kelly with questions about the Bible.

One day Tiny had invited him to go ice fishing. Brianna watched with misgivings as they drove off on a bitterly cold day. However, when they returned hours later, Eldon called Tiny a "right good chap."

"You really bond when you sit together out in the middle of an ice-covered lake," he explained. He'd even helped Tiny clean the fish, which they fried and ate for supper that evening. Brianna thought her father was a right good sport.

Kate had decided to stay for the wedding. She changed her reservations and finagled a ride with Eldon to the airport later that day. She now sat in her usual seat in the front row.

Brianna was relieved that Eldon and Kate planned to leave right after the wedding. A storm that would disrupt travel was rolling in from the Rockies. The local people had been preparing for it all week. The McLean's had moved their prize herd to a protected place. The Co-op had been busy fueling up vehicles. The local grocery store was crowded as people loaded up on bread and milk.

While the storm was menacing, Brianna looked forward to being snowed in with Tiny in the old Queen Anne house.

Now, she took a deep breath, feeling that she had wings of hope. She turned to her father. "I love you, Daddy. Thank you for being here for me." He squeezed her arm in response and she nodded to Amber. The audience's chatter stopped as soon as Amber hit the first chords on the piano and began singing.

"*Joyful, joyful we adore thee, Lord of glory, Lord of love...*"

Brianna and her father stepped forward. Her eyes locked with Tiny's and power shot between them. She had let her dark hair hang long and loose for Tiny, who now mouthed "Wow!" Red lipstick highlighted her olive skin and matched the bouquet of red velvet roses she carried. She wore pearl earrings, a gift from her father, and the necklace Tiny gave her for her birthday.

"*Hearts unfold like flowers before Thee, opening to the sun above. Melt the clouds of sin and sadness. Drive the dark of doubt away. Giver of immortal gladness, fill us with the light of day.*"

Walking up the aisle of this country church to the ageless music of Beethoven was far removed from her former soulless existence. As Amber sang out the next words, Brianna agreed with them in silent prayer.

"*All Thy works with joy surround Thee, earth and heaven reflect Thy rays. Stars and angels sing around Thee, center of unbroken praise.*"

At the front of the church, she turned to her father for a long embrace, then took Tiny's rough hand and stepped before Kelly. Amber finished the song with a flourish and came to stand at her side. She found great comfort in being surrounded by Amber, Kelly, her father and Kate on the biggest day of her life.

As she looked up at Kelly, she was startled to see sadness in his eyes. She knew he was remembering Kyle, something only the two of them would think of at this moment. The shared memory of her first love and Kelly's twin bound them together as siblings of the heart.

Shaking off the moment, Kelly smiled and began the ceremony. "Friends and neighbors, we are here today to witness and celebrate the marriage of Tiny Winger and Brianna Davis. They've asked me to keep it short, but first—."

Tiny groaned and a chuckle went through the audience.

"I know a storm is brewing and your stomachs are growling. However, I promise there is enough barbequed beef downstairs to feed the whole county. You'll have plenty of time to get home safely. And wait until you see the wedding cake. It's as pretty as the bride's dress."

Kelly frowned. "Actually, the wedding cake *looks a lot like Brianna's dress.*" The audience laughed again.

"Before these two say their sacred vows, I want to share some words from Isaiah 61."

*He remembers how much that scripture means to me,* Brianna thought.

"Please bow your heads and pray with me. Gracious heavenly Father, you have brought two souls together who were worlds apart, and yet are so right for each other. We declare in agreement with Isaiah 61 that this will be a year of the Lord's favor for them as they commit their lives to each other and to You. In Jesus' name. Amen."

He then read verse three. "To provide for those who grieve...to bestow on them a crown of beauty instead of ashes, the oil of joy instead of mourning, and the garment of praise instead of a spirit of despair.'"

Brianna stole a look at Tiny. He looked as dazed as she felt.

Looking into the audience, Kelly continued, "This is one of the most beautiful promises in the Bible. Someday I hope you hear Brianna and Tiny's testimonies, for God has brought them through hardship, mourning and despair. Today, they are proof that God keeps his hope-filled promises."

Kelly turned to the couple again. "Tiny and Brianna, in our pre-marriage meetings it was apparent how much your lives have been transformed. I believe God has a special plan for you and that you will bring new life to each other and to Cottonwood Creek. You see, marriage is more than two people in love. The best marriages are those where husbands and wives become a team, fulfilling God's purpose for their lives.

"The next chapter, Isaiah 62, begins with these words, 'You shall be called by a new name, which the mouth of the Lord will name.'

"Now, Brianna is changing her last name from Davis to Winger. However, what about Tiny? We considered this question and a decision was made. Tiny deserves to shed his nickname, which in no way reflects who he is today. From now on the man formerly known as Tiny Winger will be known as Micah Winger."

The audience stirred with this unusual news. Brianna was grateful that Kelly skirted the issue of Tiny's full name, Valentine Mikhayhu Winger. Jolina apparently named him Valentine because he was born on that holiday. Micah was her father's name. They had no clue why she'd used a Jewish spelling. Now, he had changed his legal name to Micah V. Winger.

"Tiny was named after his grandfather, Micah Monroe, an officer in the military. Micah means, 'Who is like God' in Hebrew. Now, it's time to begin calling him by his proper name. So without further ado, let's proceed with the wedding vows for Micah and Brianna."

Everything else dropped away. Brianna was in a world of two as the man formerly known as Tiny pledged to love and cherish her forever. She eagerly repeated those promises back to him. Soon, Kelly declared, "I present to you, Micah and Brianna Winger. You may kiss the bride." Applause broke out across the sanctuary.

Brianna wondered if Micah had more courage than Tiny. Would he kiss her in front of the crowded church? One of the guys leaning against the back wall put his fingers to his mouth and whistled shrilly. Others began to clap, and soon the room thundered in celebration.

Micah put his arms around Brianna, leaned her back almost to the floor, and gave her a kiss no one would forget.

Chapter 39

# Wings of Hope

The pewter-colored sky and an easterly wind signaled that the first blizzard of the season was blowing into central North Dakota.

That didn't put a damper on the wedding celebration. After the service, the line of hungry well-wishers flowed through the church and down the basement steps. Upstairs, Brianna and the man formerly known as Tiny said goodbye to her father and Kate. They sent along hugs and plates of food as the travelers hurried to catch their flights.

Then, the couple went downstairs and shook the hand of every guest. Women adjusted their clothes and fluffed their hair as they walked up to Brianna. One confided that her son had painted the angel wings on Brianna's truck. Another said to keep the shades down at Kate's place because, "there's an old fossil that drives around and looks in the neighbor's windows."

"Everyone knows the details of my life," Brianna whispered to Tiny.

The men laughed a little too loudly and mostly made the same comments. "Tiny you rascal, I mean Micah, how did you end up with this good-looking gal?" Then to Brianna, "Congratulations, Ma'am."

Many guests dropped wedding cards in a nearby basket as they stepped into the buffet line. Seats filled up at the long white tables in the fellowship hall. When people finished eating, they left to make room for another group. A number of people used a hand mic to offer good wishes, blessings or stories about Tiny.

It was after three in the afternoon when the final guest tramped up the steps and out the door. The kitchen crew, along with Kelly and Amber, remained to tidy up. The new-lyweds packed up their gifts and cards, and hauled them to the pickup. Someone had written 'Just Married' across the windshield and tied tin cans to the rear bumper.

Although Brianna wore a cape over her wedding dress, she shivered. The wind whined ominously.

Micah looked around. "We should leave before the storm hits, but I better help the others clean up so they can go home, too." *Home*, Brianna thought, *we're going home together. How strange and lovely.*

Clutching the skirt of her gown so it wouldn't get wet, she followed him back inside. The tables and chairs had been put away. Micah pulled a vacuum out of a closet and began driving it across the expansive floor.

"Hey Micah, you run a vacuum almost as well as a guy named Tiny. Do you know him?" Kelly teased. "He helps with the youth group every week."

Micah squinted in thought. "Nope. Never heard of him."

Brianna went into the kitchen and offered to help. This caused protests from Bonnie and Mavis Jackson. She had met them when they rushed to help when she broke her ankle at Kelly and Amber's wedding. Now, they led the kitchen team for her wedding.

"You just leave everything to us," Bonnie said.

"Yes, you don't want to ruin your dress," Mavis added.

"I really want to help. You've made our wedding out-standing and the least I can do is lend a hand," she ex-plained.

"Oh, let her help," Amber said, throwing a dishtowel to the bride.

*Thank you, Lord, that Amber understands.* A sweet peace filled Brianna as she dried the glass serving bowls and pickle dishes that had probably been used for count-less weddings and funerals.

***

The first snowflakes pelted the couple as they arrived at Kate's place and carried packages into the house. They had enough barbequed beef, salads, kuchen and wedding cake to last through the longest blizzard.

Then, Micah left to fill the pickup with gas before the storm and park it where the snowplow wouldn't bury it. Brianna stowed the food in the fridge, then went back to the parlor to watch for Micah. Several minutes later, he backed into the driveway so the pickup faced the street, but he didn't get out.

***

Filling the gas tank had been a lame excuse, Micah thought as he drove slowly to the gas pump. What he really needed was a few minutes to himself.

He had just married the Mango Queen and he felt like a mayonnaise jar in a pressure cooker. Being Bri's husband was a whopping big step. He was way out of his league. How could he measure up to what she was used to or what she needed?

The wedding itself was an ordeal. Standing in front of all those people like a steer in the sales ring. He had checked his zipper twice and wished he had on his green cap instead of wearing a fancy hairdo. Then, with Amber singing and Brianna and her father walking up the aisle, he knew there was no going back.

That's when he thought he'd pass out. Bill Pickle had grabbed his arm as if he was falling through the ice on Lake Audubon.

He was glad Kelly handled the business about the new name so well. He shivered to think of the ribbing he'd get if people found out his weird name. It was time to change it, to be Micah. He didn't feel like the heavyset man who had worn a brown suit and flip-flops to Kelly and Amber's wedding. Not that he liked wearing this monkey suit and necktie. Ties still reminded him of a noose. Still, as Kelly had said, he was becoming a new person.

He drove up Main Street and backed into Kate's driveway. He could see Brianna watching him through the window, but he didn't go in yet. Too many thoughts crowded his head.

Today when he spied her at the back of the church and their eyes met, he thought the sizzle between them would burn holes in the bottoms of his shoes. Then, standing next to her at the altar, he felt the earth shake, but it was only his quaking heart. He had declared his vows in a loud voice because he wanted everyone to know he meant to cherish her above all else.

His friends didn't make it easy. Man, he wished Kelly hadn't set up that open mic at the reception. "Marriage is like a deck of cards...in the beginning all you need is two hearts and a diamond. By the end you wish you had a club and a spade," one of them announced into the mic. Everyone laughed except Micah and Brianna.

Boy, he hoped they were wrong. He'd seen what his folks went through. He wanted a marriage like Amber and Kelly's. Whoever thought two people could be so much in love? Maybe, if they hung around together they could learn how to remain in love, too.

Now his bride waited for him inside the fancy old yellow house. Calm settled over him. He'd always feared Kate, but now her home would be his home. He glanced in the rear-view mirror and patted his hair. Brianna liked his new style. Then he climbed out of the pickup, eager to be with her.

***

When Micah finally came in the door with a burst of cold air, Brianna's heart soared as though she were sailing on wings of hope.

He shed his parka and snowy dress shoes. "Here we are," he said, stuffing his hands into his pants pockets.

She nodded. Her mouth felt as dry as the first time she gave a presentation. "I thought the ceremony went well."

"Yep. Kelly sure has a way with words and Amber's song was real pretty. The food was good even if we didn't have corndogs. And, I didn't see any red eye being passed around. I call that a good day."

Micah strolled toward her. "I'm glad we didn't wait until summer to get married."

*Certainly, God's favor was with us*, she thought as she glanced out the window at the snow falling in the dusky light. She pulled him close by his lapels. "I'm glad it's storming."

Micah's arms went around her and he whispered into her hair. "It looks like me and my Mango Queen will be in a world of our own for a few days."

"I'm ready for that. Come with me, I want to show you the honeymoon suite. We can turn on the fireplace and talk about everything that happened today," she said.

"Ah, talk? Sure thing," he answered. "Lead the way, Mrs. Winger."

***

Indeed, time alone in the lovely Queen Anne was a perfect way to spend a honeymoon. However, by the third day, they were getting restless. Brianna was unnerved because the streetlights stayed on all day and the windows rattled in the wind. She prowled from one snow-splattered window to another, hoping to see a break in the clouds.

"Cabin fever," Micah said. He went out to shovel snow from the porch every few hours. They ate barbequed beef and wedding cake, and placed the top layer of the cake in the freezer for their first anniversary. They took the Christmas decorations down, trucked them up two flights of steps, and stashed them in the attic.

Micah called his mother to tell her he'd gotten married. She refused to talk with her new daughter-in-law, but Micah reported that she remembered Brianna had brought her favorite doll. Before they hung up, Jolina said, "Save me some cake. I like cake."

When Brianna called California, she was thrilled to hear that her parents were getting along well. She didn't ask about the weather there because she knew the sun was shining and the orange trees would soon blossom.

However, when she called Kate, she found herself exclaiming, "It's blizzardy here!"

Kate had no sympathy. Instead, she responded, "We have a pool right outside the door." Before Brianna could feel any envy, Kate added, "But I'm not going in, I'm afraid it would take a crane to get me out."

They laughed over that and then Brianna asked, "What's that music you're playing?"

"Oh, it's a Glen Miller tune. *In the Mood.*"

"I take it you and your friend are having a good time?"

"We're enjoying a little auld lang syne," she said demurely. "However, Brianna, it's not polite to pry." *Hmm,* Brianna thought. *Maybe she won't pump me for details about the honeymoon as she did Amber.*

One evening they opened their cards, taking time to read each one aloud. Brianna recorded the cards and gifts in a notebook and wished they had a stash of thank you cards so they could respond right away.

In quiet moments, Brianna thought about this man with whom she had promised to spend her life. Micah was different from other men who had pursued her and left her feeling sad. She decided that love and lust were both four-letter words, but only love lifted you up. Without reservation, she returned the love and honor Micah gave her.

When they awoke on the fourth morning, a golden glow washed into the room. Brianna slipped out of bed and went to the window. "There are rainbows around the sun," she cried.

"Sundogs," Micah muttered. "Means there are ice crystals in the air. It's gonna get cold. It's going to be like living in a walk-in freezer."

She shivered. *How can it get colder outside?*

***

Years later, the couple would look back at their honeymoon and remember how the world seemed to stand still. For a few days, they were free to focus on each other.

Of course, their relationship wasn't all romance. That morning as she snuggled next to him, Micah leaned back with his arms behind his head, his smile revealing the gap between his front teeth.

"Bri, I'd like to have breakfast in bed this morning. Will my little wife get me some scrambled eggs and a side of bacon?"

"In your dreams," she replied.

# Chapter 40

# His & Her Businesses

After a long snowstorm and a short honeymoon, Micah and Brianna resumed their daily work schedules.

Tiny's Gym was open six days a week, from seven in the morning until seven at night. Micah's first stop each morning was to unlock the gym door. Members were on the honor system, so he didn't worry about nonpaying customers or vandals. Besides, if Maggie saw anything strange going on, she'd call him between washing someone's hair and blowing it dry.

Briana and Amber had taken over the decorating in spite of his protests. And, he thought they had too much fun doing it. Dressed in denim, they talked, laughed, and played loud music as they laid gray square tiling across the space. Of course, it wasn't really gray. It was "Pebble." He didn't argue the point.

They painted the walls "Burnt Sienna." When he told Brianna that they looked orange, she had given him a stare that would curdle milk. He didn't mention it again, but in his heart he would always think the walls were orange.

An assortment of mirrors and positive sayings covered the walls before he could veto the idea. *"Motivation is what gets you started. Habit is what keeps you going."* was strung across one wall. For their efforts, Davis Designs and Gates Insurance North had free advertising space on the wall by the door.

Brianna and Amber taped photos of Micah in the front window. The first was a picture of him, his middle bulging over his belt, as he stood with a giant soda in one hand and a bag of chips in the other. He'd lost seventy-five pounds since then and the photo embarrassed him. He'd let that go, too.

The next photo showed him looking pretty buff, although he still had a few pounds to go. Then, they had the nerve to put the photos in an ad in the *Cottonwood Times*, along with a snapshot of the remodeled space and the affordable rate.

People flocked to become members. From comments, he knew they were drawn by both his weight loss success and the uptown décor of the gym. He gave Brianna a chunk of credit for the gym's success. Every woman in town wanted to come to the classy space she'd put together.

After opening the gym for the day, he drove to Your Friendly Co-op to power up the lights, computers, and shop equipment. He'd followed the same routine since he was in high school. Back then, his father was the manager. For the last decade, he'd filled that role. It was ten after seven when he dropped the coffee grounds in the giant coffee maker and flipped the switch.

When June Miller arrived, she hustled to the backroom to bake fresh cookies and prepare breakfast sandwiches for sale. In the next half hour, a dozen people stopped by for fuel or coffee. Business would remain steady for a couple of hours and then they'd have a break until the noon rush began. During the lull, June refilled the candy section and prepared hot sliced pizza for the high school kids.

Rusty showed up at eight to open the shop. Rusty and Micah could take care of most mechanical problems. They also fixed tires, changed oil, and put in new batteries.

The convenience store and shop brought in about the same income. As far as Micah was concerned, he'd like to keep it that way, but times were changing. Vehicles were going high tech. Now you needed a computer to figure out what caused a thump under the hood. A lot of people went to Bismarck, Minot, or even the Twin Cities for car repairs. He figured the co-op would need to branch out to stay afloat.

When the morning rush was over, Micah drove to the post office to collect the day's mail before going back to the gym to work out. As he approached, two women walked out, ponytails swinging, gym bags over their shoulders. Regular customers, they smiled and greeted him.

Inside, Micah had the place to himself. Bitter cold had set in following the snowstorm, so he was extra glad he could jump on the treadmill instead of jogging his usual route along the highway. As always, his thoughts turned to Brianna.

*Bri. The Mango Queen.*

His love for her was as powerful as a 747 thundering down a runway. There would only be one woman for him. But it was more than that. They were partners in dreaming and building their lives together.

For Micah, the long years of loneliness and waiting were over.

***

Brianna's days were filled with wallpaper. Since going into business with Kate, she had learned there were many ways to update a seven-bedroom Queen Anne house. Most of them had to do with the wallpaper that covered almost every wall. She wondered if she would ever get out of wallpaper purgatory.

Their plan to open the B&B before Christmas seemed naïve now. The house was Kate's pride, the showpiece of Schulteville. And a museum of outdated décor. The wallpaper had been various shades of yellow, from banana to egg yolk, all of it mellowed and tattered with age. Plaids, stripes, cabbage roses, small flowers. It should have peeled off in long strips. Instead, she took much of it off inch by square inch.

Few rooms would remain yellow, although Kate insisted on a pattern of small yellow roses in her bedroom. The rolls lay in a heap near the mirrored closet door waiting to be hung.

As Brianna peeled wallpaper, the thought came to her that with God all things work for good. When she stayed at Kate's place after she broke her ankle at Kelly and Amber's wedding last year, she decided it was the most fascinating house she'd ever seen. She still thought so.

Now, she still did her lucrative design work online. She also spent a day or two each week on her sign business. She'd helped Amber and Micah spruce up their businesses. And she'd gotten married. *What a year it's been*, she thought.

Happy memories of her wedding day made her mind drift for a moment, before coming back to the present. Micah had helped a lot with sorting through the rules and regulations for start-up businesses. Beneath his unrefined ways, he had a natural acumen for business.

The wallpaper was difficult, but the plumbing had blindsided her. They needed to replace pipes, faucets and toilets. Plus, she wanted to add a bathroom. She was still trying to nail down a plumber, though once the cold weather arrived, Micah urged her to wait until spring for that job.

With the dearth of repair people in the area, she'd figured out how to remove wallpaper, tear out carpet, dismantle cabinets, refinish stair banisters and paint walls. Looking at her short clear-coated fingernails, Brianna moaned. In San Francisco, she mostly did computer work, visited stores with clients, held up fabric swatches, and contracted appropriate craftsmen.

Now, her perfect nails were history, but she no longer felt that her looks defined her. Instead of "there's more to me than meets the eye" her new affirmation was "with God all things are possible."

She pushed a scraper under a loose piece of wallpaper. Always the perfectionist, it was a sign of desperation that she'd paint over the wallpaper in some rooms. It was much easier than trying to tear it off. She would probably try wallpapering over some of the wallpaper next.

When she finished a section, Brianna took a break and made a trip to the turret on the third floor. Though the turret was small, it would likely be a popular rental space in the B&B. Her boldest plan for the house was to install a small bathroom in the adjacent attic.

She could already imagine the turret dressed in white muslin curtains and rain-washed green walls. She planned to replace the iron bedstead with a tall cherry wood headboard she found in the attic. A heritage quilt would cover the bed. A cozy chair tucked in the curved window area would offer a place to read or reflect. She planned to place a vase of silk sunflowers on an antique washstand.

Brianna wanted to use the space for her own private dream center. A place where she could think, pray, and look through the tall windows at the vast landscape. From the window, she could see the back of a large sign at the edge of town.

She knew what it said. "Welcome to Schulteville. We're glad you're here."

# Four Months Later

Water trickled from under a tall, crusted snowbank and joined other rivulets flowing toward the edge of town. In the middle of the yard, a snowman drooped to one side, defeated by the sun. His carrot nose had fallen out and been stolen by a passing bunny.

Brianna stopped at the edge of the street. Like a kid, she pushed snow, sand and leaves with her foot to form a dam. Soon water ran over the instep of her knee-high boot.

She had embraced her first winter like a long-lost sibling with whom she could play. In the last few months, cross-country skiing had become her go-to sport. As often as possible, she clamped on her skis and cut a trail across the prairie landscape.

She had reluctantly joined the couples bowling league, but found it was a good way to make friends. She loved a good snowball fight and skating on Cottonwood Creek. However, she gave up on ice fishing after one chilling trip with the man formerly known as Tiny.

Slogging across the street, she marveled at the miracle of spring. A robin preached a sermon from the branch of a nearby tree. Or was he calling for a mate? The honk of geese caused her to look skyward. Hundreds of geese were flying north to their summer homes. She hoped some of them would nest near Schulteville again this year.

A gentle breeze caressed her cheeks and she longed to stay outdoors. However, this morning there was no time to play. She had a batch of Fourth of July signs to box up for shipment. Opening the door of Cross Church Carpentry, she inhaled the scent of fresh-cut wood, paint, and coffee. Brianna had been relieved when Wayne and Marge came back to Schulteville at the end of January. With them in charge of the household, Brianna focused on her business.

Her sign business was doing well enough to hire helpers. One evening she had been asked to tell the youth group her story. She brought along paint and pieces of wood so the youth could make their own wall hangings. When two girls turned out to be good artists, she had hired them for the tedious work of hand-painting dozens of signs.

She also had a number of redecorating projects lined up, but her real concern was preparing the B&B for the grand opening in May. Although wallpaper was still the bane of her existence, room by room the Queen Anne was looking more refreshed.

Kate had arrived home from Arizona with a healthy glow to her skin and a spring in her step. Her cane hadn't made the trip back from Arizona. She planned to stay in Schulteville for the summer months, but to spend next winter in Arizona. Her friend would visit North Dakota during the summer.

Life in the Queen Anne seemed comfortable with all of them living there. She enjoyed morning talks with Marge and Kate. Micah and Wayne often tuned into football games, and Brianna was sure Wayne welcomed the presence of another man in the house. They all congregated in the evening to read from the Bible and offer up praise reports or prayer requests. They had often prayed for Jolina to be healed.

Then one day, they had a huge answer to prayer. While cutting fabric for curtains, Brianna had an "aha" moment. Every time she picked up a pair of scissors, she thought of Jolina stealing scissors and cutting up the drapes, sheets, or other fabric she could get into her hands.

Suddenly, Brianna knew why. If she was right, Jolina hadn't intended to do harm. No, it was because she was obsessed with making dolls. With no way to convey that, she'd simply taken what she needed.

Brianna was so sure that she was right, that she lay down her project and drove into Cottonwood City. She stopped at the Co-op to talk with Micah and then went to the mobile home.

Opening a drawer in Jolina's workroom caused her to pause for a moment. She lifted out a doll that looked surprisingly like herself. Jolina had jabbed pins into the doll. A chill went through her. Maybe her mother-in-law was dangerous. Maybe she did need to be isolated. Still, she couldn't be certain until she exposed Jolina's obsession with dolls.

She stuffed some of Jolina's dolls, fabrics, notions, and a pair of scissors in a bag and drove to Jamestown in her Blue Angel. She marched into the State Hospital full of certainty that Jolina was desperate to make more dolls. Now, a few months later, Jolina's treatment was going well and she'd soon be moving home.

Micah and Brianna often drove over to see Jolina on Sunday afternoons. During one noteworthy visit, Brianna gave Jolina a wall hanging that stated, "Who redeems your life from the pit. Who crowns you with lovingkindness and compassion. Psalm 103:4."

"Who crowns me with lovingkindness?" Jolina had asked.

"God our Father," Brianna responded gently. Somehow, she believed that the day would come when Jolina's talent for making dolls would be profitable for her. Perhaps sharing her dolls with the world would help Jolina find her way out of the darkness in which she lived.

Still, Brianna felt deeply that they needed to set up boundaries. Micah deserved some relief from caring for his mother. They both needed to focus on the art of successful marriage, something they were learning from Marge and Wayne, and Amber and Kelly.

Who would care for Jolina? The solution turned out to be a woman who had accepted a job at the local nursing home and needed a place to live. They worked out an agreement where she would live with Jolina and help care for her. Micah or Brianna would check in on her often, but the arrangement freed them to live their own lives.

They had purchased the Johnson Building and Micah was making plans to remodel it. Before work was even started on it, several people had inquired about renting space. Micah planned to move his gym into it and Brianna eventually would move her business into Cottonwood City.

One question they couldn't resolve was where to set up a permanent home. None of their options seemed right. They were welcome at Kate's place, of course, but Brianna longed for a real home of her own.

"Wherever you want to live is fine as long as we're together," Micah insisted.

All of this drifted through Brianna's mind as she boxed up the wall hangings. She'd just finished when her phone rang.

"We're all packed!" her mother announced. Her parents were going back to England. Together.

"Have a good trip," Brianna said. Her chest felt full as she thought of what it meant for her mother to give up her artsy social activities to spend time repairing her marriage.

"This time, I'll be more content and I'll really be there for Eldon. I promise. And I'll enjoy some sightseeing."

*God bless you*, Brianna thought. Her move and marriage had been a reality check for both of her parents. After seeing a counselor, they had realized that Fab had been a major source of marital stress for them.

When they confronted him about his drinking, he responded defensively and moved in with a distant cousin. They all hoped Fab would come to grips with his problems, but no one prayed more fervently than Brianna did.

She realized how close he'd come to doing serious damage to her life. The nightmare occurred less often now, and when it did, she only had to reach out for Micah's comforting presence. She was waiting for the right time to call her uncle to accountability.

Eldon and Helena's time overseas would be temporary. He planned to transfer back to the States as soon as it was feasible.

"When we move back, we're going to throw a big anniversary party for ourselves," Helena exclaimed. Brianna groaned as she considered the statement. *Thank you, God, that she's planning a party for herself rather than my wedding. Does Daddy even know about this?*

"You and Micah will attend, won't you, Darling?"

"We'll do our best to be there."

"Thank you. I'll always regret missing your wedding. By the way, thanks for sending the video. And those priceless photos! Did that newspaper publisher take them?"

"Yes, Mom."

"The gown looked so lovely on you. I wonder, will you keep it until we get back? I'd like to wear it for the anniversary party."

"Of course, I'll keep it for you. What a lovely idea."

After saying their goodbyes and after seeing her boxes loaded onto the mail truck, Brianna poured a cup of stout coffee and went to sit on the front step. Across the street, their Queen Anne home stood shining in the transparent light of the noon sun.

*Our new home.* Brianna hadn't dreamed that Kate would sell her family home. However, shortly after returning from Arizona, she had called Brianna and Micah to the parlor.

"This old house has always been a part of my life. I love it as deeply as I loved my mother and father and brother. However, I couldn't live here without Marge and Wayne's help. It certainly wouldn't have crossed my mind to open the bed and breakfast if you hadn't come into my life, Brianna.

"When I'm gone—." Kate paused for several dramatic moments, leaving Brianna and Micah wondering if she was about to share bad news. Kate's mouth twitched. "Someday I'm going to die, but meanwhile I'm going to Arizona."

They exchanged glances, wondering what she'd say next.

"It's time to make sure my old friend, Queen Anne, has a good caretaker. I want to offer the house to you. I'll give you a good price, if you'll agree that Marge, Wayne and I can live here as long as we want. And that my friend from Arizona can have a guest room in the summer."

Brianna and Micah looked at each other, eyes wide and mouths open. Perhaps they hadn't felt settled about choosing where to live because they hadn't known all of the options yet.

Brianna gasped and tears formed in her eyes. She nodded at Micah.

"Yep," Micah said. "We can work something out."

Now the yellow Queen Anne was theirs.

Brianna hadn't appreciated the color of the paint when she arrived at Cottonwood Creek the year before. Today it reminded her of sunshine, sunflowers, and the favor of the Lord that rested on her like the sunny rays that warmed the spring air.

She planned to spend the rest of her life in the yellow house, living out her Cottonwood dreams.

# Cottonwoods

-John Maddock

Alongside the river's edge,
Stand majestic cottonwood trees.

Their leaves flutter in gentle breeze,
Like dancing kites in the sky.

The lazy river,
Pays little attention
To the hungry tree roots
Channeling life to the cottonwoods.

Whose ancestors were vital to the
Native way of life.
Sturdy limbs hold eagles' nests
Atop the majestic cottonwood.

# About the Author

Gayle Larson Schuck is a North Dakota native and a graduate of Bismarck State College and the University of Mary. She worked in public information and development for 28 years and has led Bible studies for even longer. She is a member of various writers groups and enjoys reading, gardening, and spending time with her family. This is her fourth novel.

Other books by Gayle Larson Schuck

Read Gayle's blog at www.gaylelarsonschuck.com

Made in the USA
Monee, IL
08 July 2026

56550979R00134